'Go on,' said the hard voice gently. 'Open it. It won't bite.'

With unsteady fingers Julia removed the gilt paper from a long leather jewel-box, and stared wide-eyed at the string of pearls on a bed of white satin inside.

'They're lovely—quite lovely. But far too much.' How could she tell him that to her the creamy pearls looked exactly like coals of fire?

'Nonsense. You work yourself very hard for me, Julia North. These are a mere token of my appreciation,' he said matter-of-factly, and took the pearls from their box. 'Here, bend your head forward. I'll fasten them for you.'

'But these are real pearls!'

'So are the ones you wear in your ears. Besides,' he added softly, holding her eyes, 'I don't care for fakes.'

Julia went cold, unable to tear her eyes away. What did he mean? Did he guess?

COME BACK TO ME

BY

CATHERINE GEORGE

MILLS & BOON LIMITED
ETON HOUSE   18-24 PARADISE ROAD
RICHMOND   SURREY   TW9 1SR

*First published in Great Britain 1989
by Mills & Boon Limited*

© Catherine George 1989

*Australian copyright 1989
Philippine copyright 1989
This edition 1989*

ISBN 0 263 76406 0

*Set in Times Roman 10 on 12¼ pt.
01-8909-53166 C*

Made and printed in Great Britain

CHAPTER ONE

THE DAY had arrived at last. Planned for, longed for, dreaded even, now it was finally here, and absolutely nothing must go wrong. Julia walked briskly towards what she hoped was destiny. Destiny housed in a pillared Georgian building built of honey-coloured stone. It stood at the far end of a crescent where some of its neighbours were undergoing the face-lifts currently restoring the spa town to the charm of its heyday of royal patronage. But Julia had no time today for architectural charm. Her attention was concentrated on the task ahead. Today she must convince Marcus Lang, of Lang Holdings, that Julia North was exactly the person he was looking for. Miss Pennycook, his secretary and personal assistant, was about to retire after years of faultless service to Marcus Lang, and would undoubtedly be a hard act to follow. But Julia had taken great pains to learn everything she possibly could about Miss Pennycook—what she did and how she did it, and, more to the point, exactly what her replacement would be expected to do from day one.

The offices of Lang Holdings exuded prosperity. Their newly cleaned stone façade looked the acme of bygone elegance, but once Julia mounted the steps under the Doric pillars she was faced with discreet modernity in the shape of two great doors of dark, opaque glass which concealed the interior, and gave back her own reflection instead. The glimpse of herself was reassuring. From the

5

crown of her smooth black hair to the toes of her well-polished shoes she was satisfied her appearance would appeal to any man looking for a suitable secretary. It should do. She had taken a great deal of trouble to make sure the image she presented was the right one for the job. Not in the least like Miss Pennycook, of course, who was in her fifties. But, since the advertisement had specified middle twenties to middle thirties for her successor, Julia felt she was at least in with a chance.

She took in a deep breath and pushed open one of the heavy doors. She found herself in a marble-floored hall. Two attractive girls presided over a reception desk set in an alcove under a flight of marble stairs which curved upwards in a well of light. A pair of striped sofas straight from a Jane Austen drawing-room faced each other across the hall, and groups of palms in majolica jars formed a discreet screen for a row of elevator doors. Julia announced herself and her errand, then sat down as bidden on one of the sofas and waited calmly for the appointed hour. Exactly five minutes later she was asked to follow one of the receptionists. A lift took them up four floors and opened on to a thickly carpeted lobby where the girl conducted Julia to one of two panelled doors, ushering her into an office designed both to satisfy the modern demand for technology and to please the discerning eye. A spare, keen-eyed woman rose from behind her bower of machines to welcome her.

'Good afternoon,' she said pleasantly. 'My name is Pennycook. I'm Mr Lang's present secretary.'

'How do you do,' Julia smiled politely.

Miss Pennycook motioned her to a chair, then looked at her in frank appraisal for a moment or two before referring to the letter of application in front of her.

'I see you live in the town, Miss North.'

'Yes. I prefer to walk to work if possible.'

Astute eyes behind an expensive pair of spectacles held an unexpected twinkle. 'You like to keep fit?'

Julia smiled. 'Yes.' Not that she needed to keep in trim. Her life was demanding enough without formal exercise.

'Mr Lang's preference is for someone who actually lives in the town, which is why I asked,' went on Miss Pennycook. 'He believes that a long journey is an unnecessary energy drain coupled with a hard day's work.'

Julia agreed with him, but from a different point of view. A long journey meant transport, and transport meant costs, and walking to work was a means of avoiding them. Miss Pennycook asked no more questions, and pressed a button on the intercom on her desk, informing a brusque answering voice that the ten o'clock candidate had arrived.

Not even a name? Julia felt a twinge of resentment as she got up to walk to the communicating door Miss Pennycook held open for her. It gave access to a large room with what seemed like acres of carpet to cross before she arrived at the large desk where a man sat, his eyes on her face as she approached. She felt like an actress taking centre stage. The full glare of the morning sun shone on her like a spotlight, streaming in through the row of tall windows on the outer walls of a room which she realised must occupy most of the top floor of the building.

'Julia North, Mr Lang,' said Miss Pennycook, and handed Julia's letter to the man as he rose to his feet. Marcus Lang took it, gave his secretary a slight smile, and she withdrew at once to her own office, closing the door behind her.

'Please sit down,' Marcus Lang indicated the chair in front of the desk. Julia bent to put her handbag on the floor, then sat erect, ankles crossed, her gloved hands folded in her lap as she studied the man reading the information on her application form. He was a lot younger than expected; late thirties at the most, and not the most handsome man she'd ever met, by a long way. He was tall and rather loose-limbed, and the eyes trained on her before he sat down had held a faint but unmistakable look of boredom. The look in them put Julia on the defensive before they had exchanged so much as a word. He had a lot of hair, she noted, brown, streaked with grey, and his nose had been broken at some stage. He had a very wide mouth too—shut very firmly, as though he knew his own mind at all times. Which he must do, conceded Julia, if he were head of an outfit like this.

She turned her attention from the silent, absorbed man, to the room he used as an office. A vivid John Piper screen-print hung on one wall, a tranquil Cornish landscape in oils on another, and the desk was old and elegant and free of clutter. A modern console standing at right angles to it held all the electronic gadgetry she would have expected from a company dealing in telemetry and communications.

'I see you already have a job, Miss North,' stated Marcus Lang after a time.

'Yes. I work for Pennington Construction.'

'And before that you were a kindergarten teacher.'

'Yes.'

He raised his eyes to meet hers. 'Why the change of career?'

Julia was ready for this. 'I wasn't suited to teaching.'

'I see. And why do you want to change your present job?'

She looked back at him steadily. 'Several reasons. I have little hope of advancement in my present employment, and, from the point of sheer convenience, my home is much nearer Lang Holdings than Pennington Construction.'

He glanced down at her letter. 'And, of course, the salary I'm offering is considerably more than the one you earn at present.' He looked up at her deliberately. 'Or is that unimportant?'

'On the contrary, Mr Lang, it's very important.' Julia returned his look serenely, determined not to let this formidable man ruffle her.

Marcus Lang ran his eye down the list of her qualifications. 'You state you're familiar with present-day office technology, and I see you already use a word processor. Here, of course, we also use a computerised information system. And I must make it clear that my work constantly takes me to the Far East and the Arab countries, and sometimes to the States. It's essential that whoever replaces my invaluable Miss Pennycook must be capable of functioning independently. Could you do that?' he shot at her suddenly.

'Yes,' said Julia without hesitation.

Marcus Lang nodded non-committally, then went on to fire a barrage of questions at her for the next few minutes until she felt physically battered. She was immensely grateful when Miss Pennycook appeared with a coffee-tray, but rather taken aback when the other woman smiled at her and went out again at once, leaving Julia to do the honours.

Was this part of the test? wondered Julia, as she stripped off her gloves. She poured strong black coffee from a silver pot into thin china cups, handed one to Marcus Lang, then added a spoonful of sugar to her own and sat down with it, sipping the strong liquid with appreciation.

'How did you guess I take mine black, without sugar?' said the watchful man with curiosity.

Julia smiled. 'I didn't, Mr Lang. I assumed you'd add whatever you wanted, if necessary. I left the tray within reach.'

'I see. Now——' He stopped suddenly, staring at her hand. 'You said nothing in your application about being married.'

'I didn't think it necessary to say I was *Mrs* North because I'm a widow, Mr Lang,' she told him.

Marcus Lang jumped to his feet, looking irritable. 'Then why the hell didn't you say so?'

Julia damped down her angry reaction, wary of losing any slender chance she might still possess of getting the job. 'I didn't think the point was relevant, Mr Lang.'

'Do you have any children?'

She looked up at him steadily. 'No, I don't.'

Marcus Lang returned the look in silence for so long that Julia's composure suffered badly under the scrutiny. At last he gave a slight shrug and went to the communicating door, waving her through into the other office. 'Miss Pennycook will give you a test to assess your technical proficiency—and your spelling, incidentally. Or does the word processor you use run a spell-check on your finished work?'

'It can,' admitted Julia. 'But I never use it.'

He raised an eyebrow, thanked her distantly for coming, told her she would be informed in due course whether she was successful, then left her to the rigours of Miss Pennycook's proficiency test, which was merciless.

After an hour of coping with verbatim shorthand from Miss Pennycook, followed by Marcus Lang's recorded gunfire dictation from an audio machine, plus a confrontation with a different make of word processor from the one she was used to, Julia felt utterly drained by the time she rose from Miss Pennycook's ultra-modern work station and presented the finished results of her labour.

Miss Pennycook received the pages without comment, gave her a kind smile, then took the manuscript through to Marcus Lang. After a moment or two she returned and asked Julia to spare another moment or two for Mr Lang before leaving.

Quite certain she was about to be turned down flat, Julia walked across the vast room towards the desk, head held high. Marcus Lang looked up from his study of her efforts, then jumped to his feet.

'I forgot earlier, Mrs North,' he said briskly. 'Just turn towards the light, would you?'

And to Julia's surprise he picked up a Polaroid camera and took a photograph of her.

'Saves confusion,' he informed her suavely. 'I like to put a face to each application when I sift through the pile later.'

'How sensible,' said Julia, ready to strangle him with her bare hands. She gave him a polite smile. 'Thank you for seeing me, Mr Lang. Goodbye.' To her surprise he held out his hand. She took it gingerly, doubting very much if it was a sign of good-will.

'Goodbye, Mrs North.' Marcus Lang shook her hand impersonally. 'We'll let you know in a week or two.'

After he's interviewed another dozen or so eager applicants, thought Julia with resentment. She fumed in the privacy of the lift on the way down to the impressive reception area. Repulsive man! So he needed a photograph to remember her, did he! If by some miracle she got the job she'd have no trouble at all in making him remember her. She smiled humourlessly. Marcus Lang would soon learn to pick out Julia North from the rest. The lift came to a silent stop at the ground floor and she stalked across the entrance hall, her heels clicking on the marble floor. To her surprise the two receptionists gave her warm smiles as she passed them, and she went out through the great glass doors slightly mollified by the hint of sympathy in their voices as they said goodbye. No doubt they felt the same towards every candidate who went up to the lion's den on the top floor of the Lang building—amazed when anyone emerged in one piece.

Julia looked at her watch, surprised to see it was almost lunchtime. The interview had swallowed the entire morning. If Marcus Lang took that much time over every candidate it could be weeks before she even received his letter of rejection. She felt depressed, all the shining certainty of the morning gone now, tarnished by the abrasive personality of that bored, cold man she wanted so much to employ her. And if he had to take a photograph of her, why on earth hadn't he done so straight away while she was still looking her best? After that assault-course of a proficiency test in Miss Pennycook's office she'd probably looked like a shiny-nosed hag no man would even consider as his secretary.

She walked quickly along Stanhope Crescent, past the fountains in the gardens and on to the shopping centre where she had promised to meet Sue Rivers for lunch in the coffee-shop in the arcade. Sue was there before her, defending the empty chair next to her gamely until she spotted Julia.

'Well?' she demanded. 'How did it go?'

Julia flopped down in the chair, suddenly too tired to go to the counter for a sandwich. 'Gruelling.'

'I thought it might be.' Sue grinned in sympathy. 'Let me get you something to eat.'

After a salad sandwich and a large beaker of coffee Julia began to feel better, even able to laugh about the photograph. 'Did you have a photograph taken when you applied for your job, Sue?'

Sue laughed. 'Lord, no! Lowly typists are interviewed by the personnel manager. I've never even spoken to Mr Lang.'

'Lucky old you,' said Julia with feeling.

Sue was eager for details, her round, ingenuous face alight with curiosity as Julia described her lengthy catechism and the comprehensive test that had followed. Sue had no idea if this was the norm, since Miss Pennycook had been with Marcus Lang since the year dot, and all other jobs in the firm were conducted through personnel.

'Never mind,' she said kindly. 'At least you're not in desperate need of a job, Julia. I mean, you're doing OK at Pennington Construction.'

'True.' Julia jumped up. 'In which case, I'd better get back there. I'm supposed to have spent the morning at the dentist. I don't think Mr Keyes would appreciate my stab at bettering myself in another firm, somehow.'

Julia felt guilty as she hurried back to the stuffy office which seemed very uninteresting after her brush with the luxury of Lang Holdings. Mr Keyes, the chief accountant of Pennington Construction, was a martyr to his digestive system, and tended to be irritable if she was late back from lunch. Luckily she was at her desk with five minutes to spare, her fingers tapping away at top speed on the keyboard of her word-processor by the time Mr Keyes passed through her office with enquiries about her experiences of the morning. Julia was able to tell him with complete truth that they had been unpleasant, and was left in peace to catch up on the work which had inevitably accumulated in her absence.

As she walked home that evening Julia was a prey to a variety of emotions, chief of which was a strong feeling of anticlimax. She had waited for this day so long; planned and schemed and plotted for it, even used poor Sue to achieve her ends. She was racked by guilt, as usual, at the thought of the deliberate pains she'd taken to cultivate Sue's acquaintance. Richard would have been horrified at her lack of scruples. But Richard North had been a young man of exemplary character; upright, loyal and loving. And far too young to die in such an unnecessary way. Julia's throat tightened at the memory of her young husband. All set for a steady, solid career in banking, Richard North had died in a train crash only a few months after he and Julia were married. Even after six years or so Julia found it hard to believe sometimes. One moment she'd been a new bride, in love and loved; the next she was a widow, her life changed out of all recognition. And it had kept on changing, she thought grimly. Rarely for the better.

Sue Rivers had been the unsuspecting means by which Julia had hoped to change her life again. All the ambitions and desires centred on today's interview had been fired by a remark Sue had innocently let drop about the legendary Miss Pennycook's retirement. It was the precise piece of information Julia had been waiting for so patiently, getting to know Sue, who worked at Lang Holdings, with the express idea of learning about any secretarial post in the offing before the general public was informed. Not that Julia for a moment had ever aspired to the post of confidential secretary to the managing director. Never in her wildest dreams had she thought of anything so exalted. She would have worked anywhere in Lang Holdings that was open to her, as a lowly clerk or a typist in the pool. Anything, just so she could gain a foothold in the firm. Her job at Pennington Construction had merely been preparation; a place where she could practise all the skills learned at the night-school classes she had attended so doggedly in the evenings while she worked at the kindergarten during the day. But the job had never been more than a stop-gap, a kind of launching-pad from which she could aim at Lang Holdings.

One day, Julia decided, she would tell Sue Rivers everything; confess her reasons for striking up an acquaintance she knew very well puzzled the girl, because she never took Sue up on her suggestions for meeting in the evening. Julia would have liked to. She would have loved a gossip over coffee, or a trip to the cinema. But it just wasn't possible. The risk was too great. For her plan to succeed Julia knew her private life had to stay just that—as private as humanly possible.

How I hate all this secrecy, she thought grimly, then squared her shoulders as she turned into the tree-lined road of Edwardian houses where she and Richard had first set up house together. They had been so excited about having a home of their own. She sighed. It was useless to dwell on the past. Her present path had been chosen long ago, and come hell or high water she intended to stick to it now she'd come so far. If only Marcus Lang would just choose her for his secretary she'd be home and dry. But Julia had a sneaking suspicion that the head of Lang Holdings had taken a dislike to her at first sight. She could hardly blame him—the dislike was mutual. But it was such a pity. After all her scheming, and the endless pains she'd taken to transform herself into the perfect secretary, it would be tragic if she failed at the winning post just because she'd put Marcus Lang's back up by deliberately omitting the word 'widow' from her curriculum vitae.

Julia let herself in to Number Forty-seven, calling, 'I'm home!' then stood still in the hall in amazement. Propelled by a quickly withdrawn hand from the kitchen, a chubby toddler took a few tottering steps towards her, then sat down with a plop on the carpet, his face blazing with triumph as he stretched up his arms towards her.

'Sam!' cried Julia, half laughing, half crying as she snatched him up and whirled him around, hugging him tightly. 'Oh, Sam, you clever, clever boy. You walked!'

CHAPTER TWO

A YOUNG woman emerged from the kitchen, grinning, a small girl at her heels. 'Hi! He finally cracked it, Julia.'

Julia paused in the kisses she was raining on Sam's face. 'When? How?'

'He was just crawling about on the lawn after lunch, getting utterly filthy as usual, and I told him it was about time he learned to stand up and walk like Daisy. Sam gave me a dirty look, yanked himself up on the rail of the play-pen, and launched himself towards me, just as though he'd understood every word!'

Julia shifted the excited baby boy to one hip and shook her head in wonder. 'I thought he'd be crawling to school, the rate he was going on. Come on, Laura, let's have a sherry to celebrate.'

'Celebrate?' said the other girl quickly. 'You got the job?'

Julia shook her head ruefully, and described the experiences of the morning as they took glasses of sherry out to the small back lawn to enjoy the evening sunshine. Julia dumped Sam in the playpen, and Daisy obligingly climbed in with him to keep him amused for the few minutes he was likely to wait before demanding his supper.

Laura and Tristan Murray were Julia's tenants, and occupied the two upper floors of the house. During the week Laura looked after Sam along with her own daughter, Daisy. Then at weekends Julia took care of the two children while Laura and Tristan worked together in the attic. Laura painted delicate watercolours of flowers and fruit, while Tristan, who taught art at the local college of further education, indulged in his own particular passion for etching.

The arrangement worked well. The mutual interdependence of the two families functioned very smoothly, mainly because the rules were elastic, and open to last-minute rearrangement on both sides.

'You can't be sure you were unsuccessful,' said Laura, sitting cross-legged on the grass.

'Not one hundred per cent, I suppose. But there was a hiccup because I didn't state that I was a widow in my application. Marcus Lang was decidedly tetchy about it.'

'Perhaps he fancies you.'

Julia laughed. 'You've got to be joking! His interest lay solely in whether I could cope with all his space-age gadgets and function unsupervised while he goes jetting off round the world at regular intervals. The fact that I'm a woman is quite incidental.'

'What does he look like?'

'Forbidding.'

'Golly!' Laura eyed her curiously. 'Did you see his brother?'

Julia's eyes dropped. 'No. Marcus Lang occupies the heights of Olympus on the top floor of his expensive offices with only Miss Pennycook for company. I didn't run into anyone else.'

Laura was eager to hear about Miss Pennycook, whose name had come up rather a lot over the past few weeks while Julia learned everything she could from the obliging Sue about Marcus Lang's paragon of a secretary.

'I think the successful candidate, as they say, will probably be the great man's idea of a younger facsimile of the legendary Pennycook.' Julia sighed. 'Probably all the other applicants will be more experienced than me anyway. I'm comparatively new at the game.'

Laura was comfortingly sanguine about Julia's chances. 'Besides, love, I'm a firm believer in fate and all that. And if you weren't *meant* to get this job I'll eat my hat. Why else would it turn up for you, just the way you've dreamed it would?'

'That's just it—it isn't just as I dreamed. I'd have preferred something less exalted, a job I'd have more chance of getting. Secretary to the big white chief wasn't something I ever aspired to, believe me.'

A sudden roar of impatience from Sam put an end to the peaceful interlude, and Julia jumped up to take him from the playpen, coaxing him to demonstrate his new talent again for her. She let go his fat little hand and retreated, beckoning him encouragingly, and Sam staggered towards her, chuckling in delight as she swept him up in her arms and told him what a clever boy he was.

Daisy pleaded to share Sam's bath, and Laura undressed the two children while Julia changed from her tailored suit into jeans and T-shirt. When she went into the bathroom Laura was on her knees supervising a race with model dinghies to the accompaniment of much shrieking and splashing. In her ragged paint-stained denims and clinging cotton vest, Laura Murray looked too young to be the mother of anyone, with her mane of waist-length hair and bare feet, and Julia felt suddenly weary and staid as she joined in the frolics, pinning a bright smile on her face as she scrubbed Sam's sturdy little body and dried his silky dark hair. Afterwards

Laura bore Daisy off for her own supper, leaving Julia
to feed a poached egg and steamed spinach to the hungry
little boy, then afterwards cuddled him close on her lap
while she read to him about Miffy the Rabbit and Babar
the Elephant. Whether Sam understood much of it was
doubtful as yet, but he loved the nightly closeness, and
the sound of Julia's low, musical voice dramatising the
different characters. The ritual always ended with a song.
The same song. Sam regarded *The Owl and the Pussy-
Cat* as his nightcap, and refused to settle down for the
night until it was over, by which time his eyelids were
usually heavy, and Julia could lay him down in his cot
in the room next to hers.

It was a long, long time before Julia went to sleep
later that night, however much she told herself she needed
a good night's rest. Her day started early. Sam was an
angel about going to sleep at night, but woke with the
birds, brim full of energy, and Julia always went to bed
early in preparation for the mad rush of the morning.
She got up at six-thirty, whatever the weather, and bathed
and fed Sam and spent an hour just playing with him
before she got ready for work and the hand-over to
Laura. And at least three days a week she dashed home
to have lunch with him as well, unless she was meeting
Sue Rivers. Which she would go on doing, Julia decided, troubled. She never ceased to feel guilty about the
way she had deliberately cultivated the girl's acquaintance just because Sue worked for Lang Holdings. If it
weren't for Sam she would have asked Sue round for a
meal at the house long ago. But the fewer people who
knew about Sam the better, particularly if by some
miracle Marcus Lang should decide that Mrs Julia North,

widow, was worthy of the supreme honour of working for him.

Julia expected to wait for her letter of rejection for some time, but to her surprise she received a brief missive from Miss Pennycook the following Monday, after a weekend spent mainly in the park in the welcome sunshine, playing with Sam and Daisy, and trying to ignore the tension she felt over Marcus Lang's decision.

Miss Pennycook asked if Mrs North would be good enough to spare Mr Lang a few moments during her lunch hour on Thursday the twenty-eighth. He had, it seemed, reduced the candidates to a short-list, and was conducting a series of brief second interviews.

'I'm being granted another audience,' announced Julia, as she deposited Sam with Laura. 'His Eminence would like to see me again before making his final choice.'

'Sounds hopeful.' Laura thrust a handful of silver bangles up her slender arm and took charge of Sam. 'You must be in with a chance if you merit a second look.'

Julia was by no means so certain, and presented herself at Lang Holdings at the appointed time feeling, if anything, more nervous than the first occasion.

One of the receptionists was alone at the desk and greeted her with a friendly smile, telling her to go straight up to the top floor, where Miss Pennycook was waiting for her. Somehow the fact that she was assumed to know her way gave Julia a comforting little glow, and she stepped from the lift on the top floor feeling calm and prepared for the ordeal ahead. Because meeting Marcus Lang again *was* by nature of an ordeal, she admitted reluctantly. If circumstances were different she would never dream of even contemplating working for him. But as it was, she hoped passionately to be his final choice for the job.

Miss Pennycook welcomed her with a friendly smile, and pressed her to a cup of coffee from the tray which stood ready on a small table adjoining the work station where she helped Marcus Lang run his kingdom.

'Sit down, Mrs North,' she said pleasantly. 'Mr Lang has been detained a few moments, so if you don't mind perhaps you'd care to answer a few questions from me while you're waiting.'

Privately Julia doubted very much that Marcus Lang had been detained. It was only too probable that Miss Pennycook had been instructed to sound out each applicant again before her employer did the final vetting. She assured the other woman she had no objection, and drank some of the strong black coffee to help with her composure.

'You're very young to be a widow, Mrs North,' began Miss Pennycook.

Julia nodded. 'I'd been married only a few months when my husband was killed.'

'You have other family?'

'My parents both died when I was in my teens. I live in the house my husband bought when we were married, and I defray the expenses by letting part of it to a married couple with a child.'

'How very sensible.' Miss Pennycook made a rapid note, then looked up quickly. 'Have you any plans to remarry? Forgive me if this sounds personal, but Mr Lang requires this information from all the candidates.'

Julia subdued a flare of resentment, and shook her head. 'No, I have no plans to remarry.'

'In that case, should Mr Lang require it you would be free to travel with him occasionally when the need arises?'

Julia thought that one over. Tricky. But Laura could probably be relied on to take care of Sam if necessary.

'Yes, Miss Pennycook. That would be no problem.'

'Good.' The other woman turned to the intercom as it buzzed. 'Yes, Mr Lang, Mrs North is here. Shall I tell her to come in?'

This time as Julia was ushered through the connecting door into the main office she was less dazzled. There was no sunshine to blind her as she approached the great desk where Marcus Lang stood waiting for her. In her present state of nerves he seemed taller, even more formidable than before, his loose-limbed body elegant in a suit of Prince of Wales checks a shorter man would have found difficult to wear.

'Good afternoon, Mrs North,' he said quietly. 'It was good of you to give up your lunch hour to come and see me.'

Julia sat down as he waved a hand to the chair in front of the desk. 'It was preferable to asking for more time off.'

'That's what I assumed.' He looked at her for some moments without speaking. 'Have you given much thought to whether you would like to work for me, Mrs North?'

Julia looked back at him steadily, glad he had no way of knowing she had thought of nothing else, and not for just the short time since the first interview either, but for months, years almost. Sometimes it seemed her whole life had been shaped towards finding work with Lang Holdings.

'Yes,' she said. 'I've given it a great deal of thought, naturally.'

'And what are your conclusions? Is this the type of job you want? Because I must warn you that it's no sinecure. Miss Pennycook earns every penny I pay her, believe me.'

'Oh, I do.'

To Julia's surprise he smiled. And when Marcus Lang smiled, she discovered, he looked quite different—less intimidating, almost human.

'If you'll excuse me for a moment,' he said, 'I'll have a quick word with Miss Pennycook. I shan't keep you long.'

After the door had closed behind him Julia felt calmer as she was left with time to examine her surroundings in more detail, smiling wryly to herself as she pictured Marcus Lang interrogating his secretary about the candidate's answers to her questions. Why, she wondered, hadn't he asked her the questions himself? Or would that have been too personal an approach? Perhaps Marcus Lang was making it clear any association he might have with his secretary would be purely business-like. Which was just the way she wanted it.

Julia's thick dark lashes veiled her hazel eyes. It wasn't *Marcus* Lang she was interested in, after all. He was merely a means to an end. The target for her scheming was one Garrett Lang, his younger brother, trusted so implicitly, it seemed, that he'd been made finance director of Lang Holdings. Greater love hath no man, thought Julia, than to put his brother in charge of his finances. Marcus Lang was a self-made man, as all Pennington Spa knew well enough. He was one of the success stories of the town, and Garrett, the financial whizkid who was his right-hand man, was part of the story. Julia's eyes gleamed. But one chapter in the Lang saga was unknown to anyone except herself. And she intended to put her secret knowledge to good use at the first opportunity. She sobered. She was counting her chickens. She hadn't actually been given the job yet. She clasped her hands together and uttered a silent little prayer. Then she stopped short. It seemed unethical to ask divine aid for a scheme which was likely, in the long run, to cause rather a disturbance for the Lang brothers. One they really wouldn't like.

Julia tensed as Marcus Lang strode back into the room and seated himself behind the gleaming walnut expanse of his desk. She looked at his blunt-featured face, trying to keep her own expressionless, to hide the hope in her heart.

'I won't keep you in suspense any longer, Mrs North,' he said, all too aware, it seemed, of her tension. His face was impassive, but his bored eyes missed nothing. 'I feel it's pointless to make you wait until Miss Pennycook sends you a letter of acceptance. If you feel you would enjoy working for Lang Holdings, Mrs North, I'm prepared to offer you the post of confidential secretary at the salary advertised, with a six-month trial period, during which we shall learn whether we work well together. Miss Pennycook has been my mainstay for so long that you will need forbearance if sometimes I'm impatient at first. I'll do my best to proceed slowly. And of course, for the first month Miss Pennycook will remain to give you a helping hand with the ins and outs of the job.'

Julia stared at him in silence, hardly able to believe what she was hearing. Was it true? Had she really been granted the heaven-sent opportunity she'd longed for? 'Thank you, Mr Lang,' she said, after a time, fighting to keep her voice steady. 'I'm very happy to accept.'

'Good.' Marcus Lang's face relaxed a little as he rose to his feet and offered her his hand for the second time. 'Welcome to Lang Holdings, then, Mrs North. Miss Pennycook will take care of the necessary paperwork.'

Julia could hardly believe her good fortune. And Laura took one look at her face later and ran for the sherry, while Julia waltzed round the room with Sam in one arm and Daisy in the other, until she collapsed in a little heap on the floor with the children, hugging them convulsively as she told her tale of triumph.

'So I gave in my notice to Mr Keyes—who was not at all pleased—and I start at Lang Holdings on the first of the month,' she concluded, as she accepted a second glass of sherry.

Laura joined her on the floor with her own glass, twisting a lock of long curly hair pensively. 'So you made it, Julia.'

Julia shook her head. 'Not yet. But I'm on my way.'

Laura cuddled her daughter, her eyes anxious over Daisy's flaxen curls. 'Will it really be as satisfying as you think?'

'You mean revenge is a two-edged sword and all that.'

'It doesn't go with the rest of you, that's all, Julia. I just wonder if you'll go through with this plan of yours when it finally comes to the push.'

Julia stared at the other girl in astonishment. 'But of course I will! It's been the main motivation for my life ever since——' She faltered.

'Ever since Libby died,' Laura finished for her, and sighed. 'I know. And it worries me. Whatever this plan of yours entails, it can't do poor Libby any good now, and I can't help feeling it won't do you much good either, which is more to the point, since Libby's dead and you're alive. And there's Sam.'

At the sound of his name Sam clambered to his feet, teetering at Julia's elbow with an imperious look on his chubby face. 'Din-dins,' he said firmly.

The atmosphere lightened immediately.

'OK, OK,' said Julia, jumping up. 'Time for your bath, young Sam.'

'Din-dins,' he repeated doggedly, and she scooped him up, smiling at Laura reassuringly.

'I promise you Sam won't be affected, whatever I do. He's my first consideration, always.'

Laura shrugged. 'It's time you had a few other considerations, in my opinion, like getting married again, for one.'

Julia shook her head, nuzzling her face into Sam's hair. 'No way. One man in my life is quite enough, thank you very much. Two demanding males would be more than I could cope with!'

Nevertheless, as she fed Sam scrambled egg and fingers of toast later on, Laura's words kept coming back, casting a shadow over the shining triumph of earlier. Laura was wrong, of course, Julia assured herself. The last thing she needed at the moment was the added complication of a man in her life. From the moment of his birth Sam had been the only male necessary to her. Which didn't stop her from feeling a little wistful now and then when she saw Tris and Laura together, or listened to the other girls at the office making plans for the evening. Julia gave herself a little shake. Self-pity was a luxury she couldn't afford. And tonight, she thought, brightening, she was in no need of it what-soever. Marcus Lang had chosen her from all the others to work for him. Julia found it hard to keep her mind on Sam's bedtime story as she wondered what the other applicants had been like and how many there had been. Sue had hinted at dozens, but Julia felt she was entitled to feel a little bit flattered however few candidates there'd been, for the simple reason that Marcus Lang had finally singled Julia North out from the rest for the job.

She reported for work on the first day at Lang Holdings with mixed feelings, some of which were relieved at once by the news that Marcus Lang was in Hong Kong, and her first days would be spent in the company of Miss Pennycook only. Julia sent up a secret prayer of thanks when she heard the glad news, and settled down to mastering the intricacies of Miss Pennycook's work station in comparative peace. Miss Pennycook was a brisk, efficient but kind woman, who took pains to ease Julia into her new role with as little pain as possible, and in the afternoon of the first day she took her on a little tour of inspection of the various offices in the building, to introduce her to the other members of staff. In general the employees of Lang Holdings were friendly, from Sue Rivers and her colleagues in the typing pool to the marketing men and development engineers and accountants she met on the upper floors. It was only when Miss Pennycook knocked on the final door, marked G.R. Lang, that a frisson of anticipation ran down Julia's spine and her pulse quickened as she was ushered into the presence of the man who was the entire reason for her presence there in the first place.

Garrett Lang jumped up from his desk, smiling, his hand outstretched. 'So Marcus finally found someone to replace you, Miss Pennycook. We'd all begun to think his quest was hopeless.'

'This is Mrs North, Mr Garrett,' announced Miss Pennycook indulgently, her eyes warm as she returned the infectious smile.

'How do you do,' said Julia quietly, and took the proffered hand for an instant. Was *this* Garrett Lang? His hand was cool and hard, and his eyes were warm and smiling below his shiny thatch of leaf-brown hair. And he looked absurdly youthful. The physical resemblance to his elder brother was marked, but Garrett's features were more finely cut, and his nose pure Greek, and he looked as if he'd never been bored in his life. Julia smiled back, and moved away, bent on escape as Miss Pennycook asked questions about sales figures, but the arrival of a tea-tray prompted Garrett to ask the ladies to share it with him.

As Julia drank her tea she had ample opportunity to study him as he went on at length to Miss Pennycook about the new factory in the Midlands. He was a different kettle of fish from his brother altogether, she decided, less austere. Then her eyes were drawn like a magnet to a photograph on his desk. A very attractive blonde girl sat with a child on her knee and an older boy leaning against her shoulder, both children so much like Garrett Lang there could be no doubt about their parentage. She looked up to find him watching her, a smile in his eyes.

'My wife and sons,' he said with pride. 'Do you have any children, Mrs North?'

'No,' said Julia, and rose quickly as Miss Pennycook prepared to depart.

'I hope you'll be very happy here at Lang Holdings, Mrs North,' Garrett Lang said warmly, as he opened the door for them. 'If you have any problems I can deal with, don't hesitate to ask.'

'Thank you, Mr Lang.' She gave him a composed little smile. 'You're very kind.'

She was very thoughtful indeed as she followed Miss Pennycook back to the penthouse offices. So she'd met Garrett Lang at last. And he was a far cry from the ogre she'd built up in her mind for so long.

'Mr Garrett meant what he said,' Miss Pennycook assured her as they returned to the intricacies of the computerised filing system. 'When I'm gone he's the best person to ask if you need help. Only in Mr Lang's absences, of course. Very little goes on in this building, or indeed in any other of the holdings, that escapes Mr Lang.'

Privately Julia felt her new boss sounded like a giant spider in the middle of an equally gigantic web, and she was not looking forward to his return. It was rather nice working alone with Miss Pennycook, who was as kind and encouraging as she was efficient and intelligent, and Julia grew fond of her very quickly. But when Julia arrived at her desk a few days later, slightly early as always, Marcus Lang was leaning against the tall window behind it, looking down on the early-morning bustle as Pennington's business life got under way for the day.

The tall, loose-limbed figure turned as Julia closed the door behind her and bade her employer a quiet 'Good morning.'

Marcus Lang looked at her for a moment without speaking, then gave her a brief smile. 'Good morning,

Mrs North. How are you enjoying life at Lang Holdings?'

'Very much.' Julia hung her jacket in the cupboard kept for the purpose, and took the covers from the various pieces of machinery on the work station. 'Everyone's been very kind and helpful. Particularly Miss Pennycook, of course,' she added. 'Her help has been invaluable. I shall miss her.'

'So shall I.' His eyes remained on her face. 'But I'm sure you'll prove to be a more than adequate replacement, Mrs North.'

Adequate, thought Julia with distaste. 'I'll do my best,' she said crisply. 'Miss Pennycook has a dental appointment this morning, by the way, Mr Lang. She won't be in until after lunch.'

'Then I suggest you come through to my office and we'll make a start on that rather daunting pile of paperwork decorating my desk.'

She followed him through into the main office, feeling nervous. Odd really, she thought. All her energies had been channelled into the idea of just being here, part of the workforce, her actual job a sort of accessory to her main aim. But now she was about to go over the top and get in the firing line, and she had an idea Marcus Lang would be merciless with anything less than perfection in the work presented to him. For one thing, he was one of those rare men who could dictate at speed without repeating himself, and, despite all the technology at his command, preferred to do so across the desk to a secretary rather than dictate on to a tape or use a word-processor terminal. Miss Pennycook had warned Julia of this, but it was still a bit daunting to sit there with a pencil flying across the pages of her notebook to keep up with a man who never seemed to need a pause for breath.

By the time Julia returned to her own office she was shattered. And she had an idea Marcus Lang knew it, and was amused. And to add to her joys Miss Pennycook rang later in the morning to say she had a jaw infection and had been ordered off work for a few days while she took a course of antibiotics.

'Bad luck,' said Marcus Lang, and looked Julia in the eye after she'd delivered her message. 'Can you cope?'

'Yes,' said Julia.

'Good.'

He returned to the report in front of him, apparently losing interest in her at once, and Julia retreated, ruffled, to her sanctum. The man was an automaton—probably had microchips instead of feelings. She returned to the fray with renewed concentration, determined to show him she was up to anything he threw at her, and looked up with absent eyes when he appeared at her elbow later to ask her if she intended having lunch.

'Lunch?' she said blankly.

'Yes. You know—food,' said Marcus Lang, apparently amused again. 'It's nearly one-thirty.'

Julia turned back to her keyboard. 'Oh—right. I'll just finish this first.' She typed away rapidly until she'd finished the letter on the screen, recorded it on disk to print later, then removed the disk and switched off the word-processor. To her annoyance she found her new employer was perched on the edge of the other desk, watching her.

'You're good,' he said. 'No spelling mistakes, and you corrected a bit of snarled syntax there without even thinking about it.'

'Thank you.' Julia went to the cupboard and took out her jacket. 'I'll see you this afternoon, then.'

Marcus Lang stood up as she passed him, and put a hand on her arm. She looked up at him sharply, and he took his hand away.

'Is there something wrong, Mr Lang?'

'I don't know. Not from my point of view. But I get the feeling there might be as far as you're concerned.' His eyes held hers searchingly, and with a pang Julia realised they were the same as his brother's, neither blue nor green nor grey, but a mixture of all three. 'If you have any problems don't hesitate to let me know,' he went on, and she smiled collectedly.

'Your brother said that too.'

'You've met Garrett, then.'

'Miss Pennycook introduced me to everyone here on the first day.'

'Good.' He frowned. 'It will be easier for us both, Mrs North, if we can deal amicably together.'

'Of course,' said Julia quickly, resolving to hide her hostility more successfully in future. 'I'm sure I'll be very happy here.' She gave him a deliberately diffident little smile. 'It's just that today I've been suffering a little from beginner's nerves.'

Marcus Lang's eyes lit with sudden warmth, and he laughed. 'And I've been forgetting you're not Miss Pennycook. I apologise if I've taken things at too furious a rate.'

'Not at all, Mr Lang. I'm sure I'll soon reach the necessary speed.'

He nodded. 'Yes, I'm sure too. Otherwise,' he added softly, 'I would never have given you the job.'

Not sure how to answer that, Julia took refuge in another smile and went off to buy herself a sandwich and a cup of coffee in her usual haunt. Sue was waiting for her anxiously.

'I thought you weren't coming.'

'Mr Lang's first day back at the helm, and Miss Pennycook's off sick, so it's been hectic.' Julia bit ravenously into a salad roll. 'Goodness I'm hungry! I've been working like a slave all morning. I didn't even notice it was lunchtime until Mr Lang pointed the fact out to me.'

Sue was frankly admiring, obviously of the opinion that anyone who was brave enough to work for the boss himself must be a heroine. 'I'd be terrified,' she said frankly.

Julia confessed that her own feet had been a bit cold to start with. She tucked into a doughnut with enthusiasm, then looked at enquiringly at Sue, whose round, pretty face looked troubled.

'What's up, Sue? Something wrong?'

The other girl hesitated. 'Well, when you were late I thought you weren't coming. And then I began to think that perhaps now you're Mr Lang's secretary maybe we shouldn't—well...'

'Fraternise?' said Julia, frowning. 'Don't be silly. If it weren't for you I'd never have heard of the job in the first place, Sue. I'm very grateful to you.'

'And you really think it's all right to have lunch together now and then?' asked the other girl diffidently. 'I mean, you're Mr Lang's secretary, and I'm just one of the pool.'

Julia assured her stringently that it was quite definitely all right, and began to talk about Sue's boyfriend, which was an instant diversion, since Sue confided that she was fairly sure an engagement was in the offing, which riveting topic lasted until Sue was obliged to break off to get back to work. Julia took advantage of the remainder of her lunch hour to pick up a new pair of shoes ordered for Sam, and bought a large new ball for Daisy, since Sam had somehow or other managed to puncture the old one. Afterwards she hurried back to the office, determined not to be late.

Julia was at her desk, deep in the work left over from the morning, when Marcus Lang returned from lunch. She looked up with a smile. 'Good afternoon, Mr Lang.'

'That's better,' he said in approval. 'I was beginning to think you were allergic to my presence.'

Julia flushed. 'I'm sorry, Mr Lang.'

'Don't apologise. Another of those smiles will do instead.'

She looked after him thoughtfully as he went through to his own office. Perhaps Marcus Lang wasn't as austere and withdrawn as she'd thought. And it was only common sense to keep on as good terms with him as possible for the short time she was likely to work for him. Her eyes shadowed as she considered just how short her period of employment was likely to be once she had achieved her aim. Once Marcus Lang learned her real reason for infiltrating Lang Holdings she had no illusions about his reaction. She'd be out on her ear in the blink of an eye. Julia's full mouth drooped at the prospect. Pity, really. She knew already that she could enjoy working here very much, demanding though the job might be. But her own enjoyment, she reminded herself, wasn't the object of the exercise.

Miss Pennycook was missing for the next three days, at the end of which Julia and her employer were on surprisingly good terms. Julia even began to feel she was worthy of the crown being passed on to her. The work was infinitely more interesting than her former job, and her surroundings were beyond comparison. To her alarm she even found she could have liked Garrett Lang in any other circumstances. Not that this was so strange, since from the first it was obvious that everyone in the place, from the cleaners to the directors, had a soft spot for Garrett. Their attitude towards Marcus Lang was different. Every one of his employees held him in deep respect, and in some cases, with the younger ones, in awe. He was known to give short shrift to anyone not up to their job, and demanded a high degree of efficiency in return for the salaries he paid, with the result that Julia never quite managed to lose her initial feeling of wariness towards him. This became even more pronounced when one day she failed to lay her hands on some information he wanted in five seconds flat and she felt the full force of his displeasure just the same as anyone else in the firm who fell below his rigorous standards. The experience made her chary of undergoing it a second time, though Miss Pennycook told her not to take it to heart, since Mr Lang's bark was known to be much worse than his bite.

Privately Julia doubted this very much, and resolved to avoid both bark and bite as long as humanly possible. Until, in fact, the day when she would be unable to avoid either. The day when Marcus Lang learned exactly why she had infiltrated his little empire, the moment she realised the ambition she was determined on, whatever she suffered in the process of achieving it.

CHAPTER THREE

AFTER TWO months of working for Lang Holdings through one of the hottest summers she could remember, Julia was tired but triumphant. Working for Marcus Lang, she found, was a great deal more interesting and fulfilling than anything she'd done before. To her own and Laura's surprise, although Julia was tired when she reached home every night, she was in better heart than she had been for a long time, and, demanding though each day had been, each evening she had plenty of energy left over for the equally demanding Sam, who was growing up rapidly, and beginning to talk very intelligibly, particularly when it came to his own requirements in the way of food and entertainment.

At Lang Holdings Julia started her day a little earlier, it was true, but she usually managed to finish work on time, unless there was a crisis, and got home almost an hour earlier than she had with her former job. Sam was flatteringly delighted with the arrangement, and during the hot weather Julia got in the habit of taking him into the park for a walk, or to play ball, before she began on the nightly routine of supper and bath. Usually little Daisy Murray went along too, giving the faithful Laura some well-deserved time to herself each day. Life, decided Julia, had taken a turn for the better. Sometimes she had to remind herself that her job was a means to an end, not a way of life that could continue indefinitely, however well-paid it happened to be, or however much she enjoyed it.

'You look very sunburned, Mrs North,' remarked Marcus Lang one Monday morning.

Julia smiled. 'I spent most of the time in the park or the garden over the weekend. Such amazing weather, isn't it?' Her polite, conversational tone was designed to head him off from more personal remarks, but instead of taking the hint he leaned back in his chair, ignoring the pile of work in front of him. Marcus Lang looked very tanned himself, Julia realised as she looked across at him, waiting for him to begin. He looked fit too, as though he took plenty of exercise. She wondered idly what he did in his spare time.

'What are you thinking about?' he said suddenly.

Julia coloured. 'Merely that it was time we made a start.'

The deep-set eyes, which looked decidedly blue this morning against his tanned skin, lit with an unfamiliar expression. He looked very different, in fact, Julia thought nervously. The boredom was missing. Perhaps he had a new woman in his life, she decided hopefully. Miss Pennycook had made a discreet mention of Mr Lang's divorce, just to put Julia in the picture, but no details had been forthcoming. As he lounged in his leather chair this morning, looking elegant, as usual, in a lightweight grey suit, he seemed unusually relaxed. Which was more than could be said for herself, thought Julia impatiently, as she sat, poised, waiting for him to begin on the morning's mail.

'Oddly enough, those are my sentiments exactly,' he said suddenly.

She turned cool hazel eyes blankly up to him. 'I'm sorry?'

Marcus Lang stopped lounging and sat forward in his chair, leaning his elbows on the desk, with his chin cupped in his hands as he studied her intently. 'I mean I'd like to make a start on learning something about you, how you spend your time when you leave here every day.'

Not if I can possibly avoid it, thought Julia. 'I walk, run, and read. All of it a great deal,' she said, and rustled the leaves of her notebook suggestively.

He refused to take the hint, and kept on looking at her speculatively. 'They sound like very solitary occupations. Surely an attractive lady like you has other diversions?'

'Not really.' Julia's eyes slid away from the probing gaze.

'Have you never considered remarrying?' he asked, startling her.

'No, never.'

'Are there no men in your life at all?'

'I didn't say that,' she said defensively. 'I don't have lovers, if that's what you mean, but there is a—a constant male presence in my life, just the same.'

Marcus Lang smiled rather ruefully. 'I had no doubt there would be.' He raised an eyebrow. 'Do you intend marrying him?'

Julia's instinct was to tell him it was none of his business, but instead she said quietly, 'It isn't that sort of relationship,' and to her astonishment could have sworn she detected relief in her employer's distinctive eyes. He sat looking at her in silence for so long she began to fidget under his scrutiny, her face colouring as she realised Marcus Lang's expression was quite definitely that of a male confronted by a female he finds attractive, rather than an employer dealing with an employee.

'How long have you been a widow?' he said at last, surprising her.

'Several years,' said Julia shortly, and looked away.

'And this present man of yours, have you been friendly with him all that time?'

She smiled a little. 'No. Only the last couple of years.'

Marcus smiled back with a warmth in his eyes that flustered her considerably. 'I'm not motivated by mere idle curiosity, Mrs North. What I'm trying to ask, without offending you, is whether there's anyone in your life likely to object if I asked you to act as hostess for me on certain occasions.'

Me for one, she thought, eyes narrowed, not to mention Sam. 'Precisely what would this entail, Mr Lang, and on what type of occasions?' she asked in such a businesslike manner she felt rather sorry when the warmth drained from his eyes at the overt suspicion in her voice.

'Nothing untoward, Mrs North.' He sat back in his chair, and suddenly the atmosphere was cold. 'As you know, from time to time I entertain clients to dinner. And sometimes they like to bring their wives. On these occasions I require someone present to take charge of the female side of the arrangements. Since you're no doubt aware that I no longer have a wife to fulfil this particular function, I merely wondered if you'd consider giving up an evening now and then to fill in when the occasion arises. I would pay for the privilege, of course,' he added smoothly, the boredom back in his eyes as though the warmth of a moment before had been a figment of Julia's imagination.

'Oh, in that case, of course, Mr Lang. I'll be happy to do so.' As long as she could arrange a baby-sitter. She gave him a cool, challenging look. 'But I would need to know a fair time in advance.'

'Of course. Since I expect you to organise everything, you'll know before anyone else,' he said drily, and pulled some papers towards him. 'Right. Enough time wasted, I think. Let's get on with it.'

And Julia duly got on with it, feeling just slightly regretful that the usual Marcus Lang was back in full force. The few rather disturbing moments of sexual rapport between them had vanished like snow in sunshine when she failed to greet his request with instant rapture. What did he expect? How could she have known what he had in mind? she thought resentfully, as her pencil flew over the pages in time with the rapid, lucid dictation Marcus Lang seemed to be hurling at her at more than his usual speed this morning. Julia managed to remain unruffled solely because by this time her efficiency was unquestionable. A couple of weeks under Miss Pennycook's aegis, followed by several more under her own steam, had resulted in a standard of performance up to anything Marcus Lang could possibly require.

Off to a later start than usual, the morning went on to deteriorate gradually. Julia was so deep in the intricacies of a report Marcus needed by lunchtime that she omitted to write a large portion of it on to disk on her word-processor before disaster struck in the shape of a power cut which affected their part of town for half an hour before the electricity was restored. The wonders of technology, thought Julia viciously, as she steeled herself to the re-typing of several pages of complex, esoteric terminology all over again, merely because she'd forgotten to save it on the machine as she usually did, at the end of each page. The fact that Marcus emerged from his office to stand over her for the final page or two did nothing for her frame of mind.

'My goodness,' said a cheerful voice from the doorway. 'Don't tell me you stand over the poor girl to make sure she doesn't have any lunch, Marcus?'

'Shut up, Garrett,' said Marcus, without turning round. 'I need this for this afternoon, and that confounded power cut put Mrs North back a good half-hour.'

More than that, thought Julia bitterly, as she took the last page from the printer, unwilling to admit she'd been foolish enough to lose half her text from her screen when the cut occurred.

'Thank you,' said Marcus absently, as she handed him a copy after she'd married the various pages together.

'Is that all you can say?' said Garrett, smiling at Julia. 'After a top-speed marathon like that little lot the least you can do is offer the poor girl some lunch.'

The 'poor girl' gave him a hostile glance. 'That won't be necessary, Mr Lang. I'm meeting someone.'

Garrett Lang's eyes were puzzled as they rested on her withdrawn face. 'Can't say I'm surprised, of course. Hope the chap's waited for you.'

Marcus Lang cast a black look at Julia, who knew very well she looked flushed and resentful as she collected her handbag. 'Is the conference room ready for this afternoon's meeting, Mrs North?' he barked.

Julia's colour rose even further as Garrett stared at them both in astonishment. 'Of course, Mr Lang, except for these reports, which I shall distribute on my way down. Just in case I'm a trifle late returning from lunch,' she added pointedly, looking at her watch, pleased when her barb found its target, as Marcus Lang had the grace to look a little shamefaced as he realised how late it was. Julia's usual lunch-hour was almost over, but she'd promised to go home to see Sam and was determined to keep to it, after a quick phone call to Laura to say she was on her way. 'May I use the telephone to say I've been delayed?' she asked meekly, and rejoiced inwardly as colour rose in Marcus's lean cheeks.

'You know perfectly well you're at liberty to use the damn phone as much as you like,' said Marcus irascibly, and stood his ground, frankly listening as Julia dialled her own number and said a few brief words to Laura, then turned to go, burningly aware that Garrett Lang was quite obviously fascinated by the little interchange.

'I'll see you later, then,' said Julia, as Garrett sprang to open the door for her.

'Take the rest of the afternoon off,' ordered Marcus curtly.

Julia was sorely tempted, but she knew time off would only mean twice as much to get through the next day. 'No, thank you, Mr Lang,' she said in a martyred tone. 'I'll just take my lunch break, then get back to work as usual.'

'Let me drive you wherever it is you want to go,' offered Garrett.

Julia opened her mouth to refuse, then thanked him instead. 'That's very kind of you, Mr Lang. A lift would be most welcome in the circumstances.'

As Garrett ushered her from the room Julia controlled the urge to scuttle away at top speed from the stormy look on Marcus Lang's face as he watched his brother escort her to the stairs. Garrett's grin as he waved airily at Marcus seemed unlikely to improve matters either, she thought, as they went down to the conference room on the way out, but that couldn't be helped. This, as it happened, was a golden opportunity. After the stroke of luck in actually getting the job at Lang Holdings Julia had decided not to push her luck afterwards for a while, to tread water until the time seemed right to proceed further with her aim to get to know Garrett Lang. She was glad she'd been patient. Now neither Garrett nor Marcus Lang could accuse her of engineering the present situation. She smiled up at Garrett as he helped her distribute the reports on the long, gleaming conference table. 'It's very kind of you, Mr Lang.'

'My pleasure,' he assured her as they went down in the lift to the basement garage. 'Only too happy to help.'

'I feel a bit guilty about accepting a lift, since it's such a short distance,' said Julia as they arrived in the garage, 'but since I really must be back by three a car-ride's a godsend.'

'You don't have a car?' he asked, as he led her to the Audi coupé next to his brother's Ferrari.

'No.' A car was a luxury Julia had never been able to afford. 'I like to walk to work. If you'll just drop me in Chester Square, Mr Lang, that'll be just fine.'

They chatted pleasantly on impersonal subjects on the short drive, during which it was easy for Julia to see what made Garrett Lang so popular with everyone. Unlike his more introverted brother, Garrett possessed a friendliness she found she responded to against her will. So much so that she was glad when the car drew up under the sticky lime trees in Chester Square and she could escape from the presence of a man whose very name before she met him had acted on her like a red rag to a bull.

Julia made sure Garrett Lang's car was well out of sight before she turned down Chester Road and ran home for the brief, energetic half-hour she could spare for Sam before dashing back to the office again. Sam was surprisingly clingy when the time came for her to leave, and it took all Julia's effort of will to disengage the hot, sweaty little hands from around her neck and kiss him goodbye.

'I'll be home again soon,' she promised him, and he hugged her hard, giving her a smacking, sloppy kiss which she returned lovingly.

'Bring sweeties?' he enquired hopefully, as Laura took his hand.

'No fear,' said Julia firmly. 'I'll bring you a beautiful big orange, and we'll peel it together after you've had your supper. OK?'

Sam beamed, and waved his chubby hand at her.

'Bad morning?' said Laura.

'Odd, rather. I'll tell you more when I have time. See you later.'

Julia hurried through the crowded sunlit streets on her way back, fairly sprinting along the crescent as Lang Holdings came in sight. She was still out of breath when she arrived at her desk, and felt sticky and hot and thoroughly out of sorts as she began on her afternoon stint. She worked rapidly, making the most of the peace and quiet due to Marcus Lang's absence at his meeting a floor below. Sometimes he required her to sit in on a meeting and take notes, but today he had elected to make notes himself and give them to her afterwards. Marcus Lang not only dictated lucid, grammatical prose, he also wrote legible notes in a flowing bold hand Julia had no trouble in reading. All in all, she admitted secretly, when she broke off to enjoy a cup of tea later, Marcus Lang was a good man to work for. Demanding, it was true, but not unreasonable, and with an impersonal manner she very much appreciated. Not that his manner earlier could have been described as impersonal at all, now she came to think of it. In fact for a moment or two he had been so friendly he'd almost frightened her. The look in his eye might have been one she hadn't seen in a long time, but she'd recognised it, just the same. It had been a man/woman sort of look, and she had responded to it rather too eagerly for her own peace of mind. And when she'd implied that she had a lunch date Marcus had looked distinctly put out. Julia stared absently into her cup, remembering the look on her employer's hard face when his brother had suggested giving her a lift. Unless she were imagining things, she could have sworn he looked not only angry but jealous. She sat up straight, blinking. What on earth was the matter with her? Fantasising about Marcus Lang would get her nowhere. It was Garrett she had to concentrate on.

Julia sighed, depressed. In any other circumstances she would be perfectly happy to carry on working for Lang Holdings as long as her services were required. But she had come here with only one purpose in mind—revenge. And, two-edged sword though it was known to be, she was quite prepared to risk getting hurt as long as Garrett Lang could be made to suffer simultaneously.

It was almost five before Marcus strode into the office, looking hot and irritable, his shirt clinging damply to his broad chest, his jacket over one arm, and an ominous bundle of notes in his hand. Julia regarded them without pleasure.

'Don't worry, I'm not asking you to start on this lot tonight,' he assured her. 'You'll have plenty of time to yourself tomorrow, I shall be in London.'

'When will you be back, Mr Lang?' asked Julia, consulting the computer beside her. 'You have no appointments tomorrow, fortunately, and nothing on Wednesday I can't rearrange.'

'I know, I know.' He raised a heavy eyebrow at her. 'I had sufficient foresight to consult the oracle in your absence, don't worry, before I arranged the trip.'

'Of course, Mr Lang,' murmured Julia, and began to tidy the office, preparatory to departure. Marcus stood looking at her.

'How much notice do you need?' he asked abruptly.

Her stomach lurched. 'Notice?' she asked warily.

'To arrange, and grace with your presence, one of those business dinners I mentioned this morning.'

Julia thought for a moment. 'Two days should be sufficient, Mr Lang.'

'Then book a table for six at the Chesterton for Friday. Give instructions for the chef to pull out all the stops. Send a formal invitation to Mr and Mrs Dwight McAllister at the Chesterton Hotel, and I suppose you'd better send one to Claire while you're at it.'

'Claire?'

'My sister-in-law,' said Marcus patiently. 'She and Garrett will make up the six.'

'I'll see to it first thing in the morning,' said Julia, and gave him a polite little smile. 'Goodnight, Mr Lang.'

'Wait a minute.' Marcus took a cheque-book from his jacket, and hunted through his pockets for a pen. He scribbled quickly on a cheque, tore it off and handed it to her. 'That should cover it, I think.'

Julia frowned, puzzled, as she read the amount on the cheque. 'Do I need to pay in advance at the Chesterton, Mr Lang?'

He picked up his jacket, a smile in his eyes Julia disliked on sight. 'No, Mrs North. The cheque is for your overtime and a dress. Nancy McAllister is a clothes-horse, and Claire has impeccable taste, so I imagine you'll feel happier if you're dressed in keeping. Not,' he added hurriedly, as Julia's face went rigid with affront, 'that you ever look anything but perfect, here at the office. My intention was to avoid any expense you might feel obligated to go to on my account by way of a dress suitable for the Chesterton.'

'How thoughtful of you, Mr Lang,' said Julia stonily. 'Thank you.'

She left quickly before she was tempted to throw his cheque at him and tell him exactly what he could do with his dinner and his notes and his rotten job included, and walked home at a pace more suited to a frosty winter's day than a languid summer evening where no breath of air stirred the sycamore trees along Chester Road.

'Lord, you look hot,' said Laura with sympathy. 'Come and drink some of the ginger beer I made.'

'At least a pint of it, just for starters,' said Julia, scooping up the clamouring Sam.

'Auntie Julia, Sam hit me,' Daisy informed her, displaying a bruise on her small brown arm.

'Did you hit Daisy?' demanded Julia, looking sternly at the little boy.

He nodded proudly. 'Bam!' he explained by way of illustration. 'Daisy naughty.'

'Daisy's never naughty. You're the naughty one,' Julia told him sternly. And I love you so much it hurts, she added silently, as she made him kiss Daisy's arm better before she let him toddle off with the little girl to the sandpit at the end of the garden.

'Your day failed to improve, I take it?' asked Laura, as they subsided into tattered deck-chairs on the lawn.

'No,' said Julia with an explosive sigh, and explained about the dinner arrangement and the cheque. 'How I wish I already owned a drop-dead sort of dress, so I could have refused his cheque with icy disdain. But I don't, so I took it.' She showed it to Laura, who whistled in admiration.

'Enough for three dresses there, Julia!'

'Ah, but part of it's to reimburse me for my valuable time, don't forget. Overtime, in fact.' Julia looked across at Laura questioningly. 'Will the extra baby-sitting bit be all right?'

Laura smiled. 'Of course. Besides, it's not really baby-sitting, is it? All I have to do is switch on the baby intercom, and pop down here now and again to check up. And you know Sam rarely wakes up once he's gone off to sleep.'

'I know.' Julia sighed. 'But I'd hate you to think I was taking advantage of you, Laura.'

'Enough of that, landlady. Our arrangement works well on both sides, don't forget.'

'And I'll pay you some of the overtime I get too,' said Julia, brightening, and brushed aside Laura's indignant protests. 'Fair's fair, Mrs Murray. Besides, think of all the new paints you can buy!'

Julia was glad of the respite while Marcus Lang was away. He left instructions for her to deal with as much as she could on her own, which was a fair amount by this time, as Julia grew steadily more familiar with the running of his small empire, and Garrett Lang took up any time she had left over. His own secretary was off sick for a day or two, and when he asked Julia if she could lend a hand she agreed readily, glad of the opportunity to further her ambitions in his direction.

'I gather you're coming to the dinner tomorrow night,' remarked Garrett, as she got up to return to her office.

'Yes, Mr Lang, it's all arranged. You received the formal invitation, I trust?'

'Yes, Mrs North. Or will you let me call you Julia?' His grin was engaging, but Julia shook her head. While Marcus Lang referred to her punctiliously as 'Mrs North' it seemed unwise to allow anyone else the use of her first name.

'I think it's best to keep to keep to the status quo, Mr Lang.'

'My intentions are of the purest, you know.' Again the flash of perfect white teeth. 'I love my wife, honest.' The chameleon eyes widened in surprise. 'Why, what did I say?'

'Nothing,' said Julia hurriedly, and forced herself to smile. 'I'll return these to you before I leave.' She left Garrett staring at her blankly as she whisked herself from his office with a haste very uncharacteristic of his brother's self-contained Mrs North.

She stared blindly at her impeccable shorthand as she hammered away on her keyboard, one half of her mind automatically transcribing the symbols into well-turned phrases on the screen, the other sick with reaction over the fact that Garrett Lang loved his wife.

'You're busy, I see,' said a familiar voice, as she printed the last of Garrett's letters, and her heart gave an entirely unexpected thump in her chest. She took time to arrange a polite smile of welcome on her face before turning to face Marcus, who was leaning in the connecting doorway between their offices, looking rather less together than usual, with his tie loosened at his open collar.

'Why, good afternoon, Mr Lang. I wasn't expecting you back until tomorrow.' Julia felt utterly dismayed by the pleasure she felt at the sight of of the tall, rangy figure of her employer.

'I got through quicker than I expected.' Those same chameleon Lang eyes looked at her searchingly. 'I trust my brother hasn't taken advantage of you too much, Mrs North. You look tired.'

'It's the heat,' she said quickly, and closed the file containing his brother's mail. 'Would you like some tea?'

Marcus sighed, rotating his head wearily on his neck. 'What I'd really like is a very large gin with a very large tonic and a whole bucketful of ice. But after a tussle with the M25, the M4 and the last few miles into Pennington behind a convoy of articulated lorries I might never manage the drive home if I yielded to temptation.'

'Take a taxi, then, or get your brother to drop you off,' said Julia practically.

Marcus stared at her. 'You know, that's an absolutely brilliant idea! I will. Join me.'

Julia shook her head. 'No, thank you, Mr Lang. I must be on my way.'

He narrowed his eyes as he watched her collect her belongings. 'Is there someone at home likely to chastise you severely if you don't arrive on time every day?'

She smiled involuntarily as she thought of Sam. 'Not exactly, but I like to get away on time whenever possible. I don't mind working late if necessary,' she added hurriedly. 'But otherwise——'

'You mean a quiet drink with me in my office for five minutes isn't worth a telephone call to whoever you have waiting for you?' There was no malice or sarcasm in his voice, and Julia met the questioning eyes thoughtfully. Laura wouldn't mind an extra ten minutes, she knew. And Sam, fortunately, hadn't learned to tell the time yet.

'Very well, Mr Lang.' She smiled. 'I can't say the idea of a long, cold drink is exactly anathema to me, either. So if you'll give me a minute to phone——' She waited pointedly, and Marcus gave her a rather wry smile and went into his own office and closed the door very deliberately.

Laura raised no objections, as expected. 'Sam and Daisy are making a sort of castle in the sandpit. They'll be perfectly happy for a while yet. But be warned—Sam's really filthy tonight.'

'Who cares? Thanks, love, see you anon.'

Marcus kept a refrigerator in his office, discreetly disguised as a mahogany cabinet. 'A bit kitsch, I suppose,' he said, smiling, as he listed its contents to Julia. 'But a lot of my associates seem to expect a drink on tap, and tonight, for once, I'm in full agreement.'

She accepted the tall, ice-filled glass of gin and tonic with appreciation, smiling when Marcus apologised for the absence of fresh lemon slices. 'This is an unexpected treat just as it is, thank you.' She sipped with pleasure. 'Mm, perfect.'

Marcus took off his jacket and subsided into his leather chair, yawning. 'Lord—sorry. It was a hot drive back this afternoon.'

'Was your trip successful?'

'I think so. Quite a thriving little concern, but the owner wants to retire. It calls loudly to my entrepreneurial instincts.'

Which, as Julia knew first-hand, were almost infallible. 'Is the Mr McAllister you're entertaining tomorrow night concerned with it in any way?' she asked.

'No, just a friend. I met him in the States once, and we've kept in touch ever since. He married recently—in fact he's on his honeymoon.' Marcus smiled. 'That's why I wanted everything to be top-notch as far as the evening's concerned.'

Julia got up to find a typed sheet on his desk among the other paperwork waiting for his attention. 'The Chesterton gave me a choice of several dishes the chef does only by special request. I asked if at least three could be available, and as long as I ring them first thing in the morning you can have any of them you want.'

Instead of looking at the list Marcus stared at Julia. 'You're a marvel, Mrs North. Have another drink.'

Julia shook her head. 'I don't drink very much. Another one and I probably wouldn't be able to walk home.'

'Then share my taxi,' he said promptly.

She looked at her watch, then finished her drink. 'No, thanks, Mr Lang. I must be going. Unless there's anything more you'd like me to do?'

He nodded. 'Just one thing. Did you buy a dress?'

Julia felt guilty. 'No, I'm afraid I didn't. There just hasn't been time.'

He looked at her steadily. 'Then I suggest that you start looking for something first thing in the morning, and don't come in until you find it. If you arrive empty-handed I'll send you straight back out again.'

The changeable eyes were smiling, but something in them warned Julia that he meant exactly what he said.

'Very well, Mr Lang. Actually, I was intending to look for something in my lunch hour,' she added.

He scribbled something on a sheet from his memo pad and came round the desk to give it to her. 'Go to this place and ask for Madame Resnais. She'll find something to suit you.'

Julia took the paper from him without looking at it, privately resolving to go exactly where she liked to buy a dress.

'I'll give Danielle a ring in the morning,' said Marcus, reading her mind, 'tell her you're coming in.'

'You're very kind,' said Julia woodenly. 'Goodnight, Mr Lang.'

He reached out and raised her chin with one finger, looking down into her startled face with an unsettling smile. 'Would you laugh at me if I told you I'd missed you these past few days?'

'No,' she managed in a strangled voice, unable to look away.

'I have, you know.' His voice was very soft and deep, utterly unlike the crisp, businesslike tones she was used to, and Julia pulled away, smiling uncertainly.

'I really must go,' she said breathlessly, and he moved back, his eyes gleaming.

'Then I suppose I must let you. Goodnight, Julia.' One eyebrow rose in response to her swift reaction. 'I hoped that if you're to play hostess for me tomorrow night you might unbend enough to let me use your first name.'

'Of course. You pay me, Mr Lang, you're entitled to call me what you want,' said Julia sweetly. 'Thanks for the drink.'

CHAPTER FOUR

JULIA met with a frosty reception when she arrived in her office at eight-thirty the following morning.

'I told you to go shopping first,' Marcus said when he saw her, not even bothering to say good morning.

'I am,' Julia assured him. 'Good morning, Mr Lang. I fully intend carrying out your instructions, I promise, but since Madame Resnais is unlikely to open her premises before nine-thirty at the earliest I thought we might get a little work done before then, including letting the Chesterton know your choice of dishes before I go out.'

Marcus Lang rubbed his chin ruefully, then shook his head. 'I give in, Mrs North. And while we're on the subject, I shan't use your given name without freely given permission on your part, scout's honour. I pay you for working for me, nothing else.'

She suddenly felt petty. 'Of course you may call me Julia, Mr Lang. Shall we have some coffee before we start?'

Marcus accepted her olive branch in the the spirit it was intended, and they worked steadily together for half an hour before he called a halt.

'Right, that's enough. Now make yourself scarce— and don't come back without the gold bag Danielle uses to package her creations.' He grinned unexpectedly. 'I should warn you, it's one I know very well.'

The divorced wife, no doubt, thought Julia, conscious of distaste at the thought of a dress from the shop the ex-Mrs Lang patronised.

'My sister buys her clothes there,' said Marcus, apparently mind-reading again. 'Not at the moment, she's expecting a baby. But until she got married last year I was painfully familiar with that particular gold bag of Danielle's, I assure you, not to mention the bills!'

Julia smiled at him, then gathered up the mail. 'I promise I'll carry out your instructions to the letter, Mr Lang.'

'If the money I gave you isn't enough for whatever Danielle thinks suitable, tell her to charge it to me.'

Was he serious? thought Julia incredulously. She thanked him politely but assured him she was unlikely to need any more money for just one dress. As she went down in the lift she brooded on the extravagant sum he'd given her, thinking of all the other things she could have bought with it. Like new shoes for Sam, who grew out of them almost by the month. But it was Marcus Lang's money, she reminded herself, in which case she felt duty bound to spend all of it, if necessary, on a dress she was unlikely to wear more than once or twice. On the other hand, it would be nice, just for once, to be extravagant, particularly when someone else was footing the bill. Also, if she were honest, her confidence could do with the boost in the company of two women who were certain to be stunningly dressed. Julia's eyes shadowed at the thought of the identity of one of the other female guests. It would be very interesting to meet Claire Lang.

To Julia's surprise Danielle Resnais proved to be a lady of at least fifty, and possibly more. The Frenchwoman was pencil-thin and almost frighteningly elegant, but very charming and helpful even before Julia mentioned Marcus Lang's name, as instructed.

'So you are Monsieur Lang's new secretary,' said Madame Resnais in surprise. 'But you are not much like the formidable Miss Pennycook. You are so young!'

Julia assured her she was all of twenty-six, and rarely felt very young at all these days.

'Then you shall have a dress to make you feel young, *ma chère*.' The bright black eyes of Danielle Resnais were wise and frankly sympathetic as she ran them over Julia's serviceable navy cotton dress.

'It's only a dinner party,' said Julia hastily. 'I don't have much use for anything elaborate.'

Madame Resnais laughed and beckoned to a hovering girl, gave her a few quick instructions, then bade Julia sit down on one of the small gilt chairs dotted about the midnight blue carpet, insisting she drink some coffee while she looked at dresses. It seemed churlish to refuse, and Julia sat obediently while several dresses were brought for her approval, startled by a sudden pang of acquisitiveness as she looked at the silks and chiffons held up for her inspection.

'Something light and airy for this last burst of summer, *non*?' said Madame, and held up a a dress in creamy pink crêpe-de-Chine. 'Very thirties, *n'est-ce pas*? I adore this fabric—so fluid, so graceful.'

And so expensive, thought Julia, as the dress was slipped over her head. She looked at herself in the mirror in silence. The dress was a miracle. It skimmed rather than clung, left her tanned throat and arms bare, and she fancied the subtle colour of the matt fabric added a glow to her skin, an ebony sheen to her hair.

'It's nice, isn't it?' she said, colouring, realising she'd been staring at her reflection rather a long time.

Madame Resnais nodded indulgently. 'So English, the understatement. You look ravishing, my child, not this lukewarm "nice" of yours.'

But perfect though Julia felt the dress was, Madame refused to let her go until she had tried on others just to make sure there was nothing else she preferred. Black-dotted white voile was followed in turn by jade chiffon, but in the end it was agreed by everyone present that the blush-pink crêpe-de-Chine was the one.

'Shoes?' asked Madame, while Julia wrote a cheque.

Julia's heart sank. She had nothing suitable, she knew, and admitted it. Madame advised a visit to a shop Julia never patronised for reasons of economy rather than choice.

'It is their end-of-season sale,' said Madame firmly. 'Tell them I sent you.'

Not sure whether it was the name of Madame Resnais, or merely her lucky day, Julia found a pair of frankly frivolous shoes in glacé kid, reduced to a price she could well afford from the remainder of Marcus's cheque, and still leave enough to pay Laura a generous amount for her extra baby-sitting services.

'You found something, then,' said Marcus, when she returned to her office.

With a demure smile Julia displayed the gold bag with the name 'Danielle' written in black script across it. 'Yes, I did. Thank you.'

'Not at all, Julia.' He smiled mockingly. 'After all, if you were obliged to wear a uniform I'd have to provide it, wouldn't I?'

Julia felt doubtful about this piece of sophistry, but stowed away her spoils in her cupboard, and prepared to devote the rest of the day to the normal work she was paid for, only to find that she was ordered to take the afternoon off.

'But, Mr Lang——' she began, casting an eye at her overflowing in-basket.

'But nothing,' he said swiftly. He leaned indolently in the connecting doorway, his eyes gleaming green today as they smiled lazily at her. 'Do whatever you must until lunchtime, then beat it, Mrs North. I shall send a taxi for Julia at seven-thirty tonight, and will expect her to look rested and ready to contribute to the sparkling conversation of my dinner-table.'

Julia sat down at her work station, giving him a wry look. 'I'm not sure about the sparkling bit, Mr Lang. I'm not a very social animal, I'm afraid.'

'Just be yourself.' He pushed himself away from the door and turned back into his own room, pausing for a moment. 'If it's any consolation to you, I'm not much for social gatherings myself. We can hold hands and comfort ourselves with our mutual shortcomings if the going gets rough.'

Julia stared after the tall, loose-limbed figure as it strolled out of sight into the main office. Hold hands, indeed! He'd better not harbour any thoughts of fun and games after the dinner party! Then her sense of humour revived, jeering at her for reading too much into his casual comment. Marcus Lang was simply being friendly for once, to put her in the right frame of mind for the evening, nothing more. After which Julia sensibly dismissed him from her thoughts and concentrated on getting as much work done as possible before lunch, to make up for the time she was obliged to take off for the rest of the afternoon.

'You look amazing!' said Laura in admiration when she wandered into Julia's bedroom to inspect the new dress. 'My goodness, how much did that dress cost?'

Julia shuddered. 'Don't let's think about it. I just hope nothing happens to it during dinner.'

'Why?' Laura chuckled. 'It doesn't disappear back to Danielle's on the stroke of midnight, I assume?'

Julia twisted round to examine her back view in the mirror. 'No. But it doesn't feel like mine, somehow. Which is hardly surprising,' she added, 'since Marcus Lang paid for it.'

'Sounds terribly naughty!'

'Believe me, Laura, if I'd possessed anything remotely suitable I'd never have taken the money,' said Julia with feeling. 'What do you think of my hair?'

Laura nodded in approval. 'I like that little pearl clip thing catching it back at one side. But brush the other side a little more on to your cheek—that's right. I like it.'

Julia patronised a hairdresser only when her hair actually needed cutting, and had washed it herself for the occasion, begrudging money spent on an effect she could achieve just as well at home, since her thick hair fell straight to just below her ears, where it was skilfully cut to curve inwards at the ends. The money saved on her hair had been spent on stockings and a new lipstick, and when Julia gave a final glance at her reflection she shrugged, making a face at herself.

'Right, that's it—the best I can do. Lib's brooch in my hair, Mother's pearls in my ears, Marcus Lang's dress and shoes——'

'And my little evening purse, if you want,' put in Laura, taking a hand from behind her back to proffer a small pouch embroidered with seed pearls. 'I thought you'd be wearing the pearl earrings, so perhaps this will do.'

Julia gave her a delighted hug. 'Laura, you angel! I'll take great care of it. Tris gave you this, no doubt?'

Laura nodded. 'Found it in an antique shop when he was in Bath that time. By the way, how did Sam go down tonight?'

'The little monkey seemed to know something was up. I had to read an extra story and sing *The Owl and the Pussy-Cat* all the way through twice, but I think he's doggo now.' Julia smiled anxiously. 'I hope he stays like it for you, Laura.'

'Of course he will.' Laura peered from the window, then ran for the door before the bell could ring. 'Your taxi, Julia,' she said, coming back. 'Off you go. Enjoy yourself—and if they serve crêpes Suzette bring me back a doggy-bag!'

The Chesterton was Pennington's only five-star hotel, and Julia alighted from the taxi in front of its pillared entrance feeling tense with nerves. To her relief the familiar figure of Marcus Lang emerged to meet her at once, looking very attractive in a dinner jacket. Julia felt suddenly uncertain about her dress. No mention of black tie had been made on the invitations. No doubt the Langs felt it unnecessary to state the obvious.

But any doubts she had were dispelled immediately as Marcus took her hand and looked at her with an admiration completely untempered by the boredom which so often marred the expression in his eyes.

'Good evening, Julia. How very charming you look.'

'Thank you,' she said, her confidence shored up instantly. 'Have the others arrived yet?'

'No. I thought we'd have a quiet drink on our own before they come.' He led her into a small, crowded bar at the foot of the main staircase, where muted music soothed her tension away as Marcus seated her on a small velvet sofa and ordered champagne cocktails from the waiter after consulting Julia. The last time she'd tasted champagne in any form at all had been on her wedding day, she thought with a pang, then closed a mental door firmly on her memories, and sipped her drink with frank enjoyment.

'Lovely,' she said, and smiled up at Marcus. 'I've never tasted one of these before, Mr Lang.'

He leaned back beside her on the small sofa, smiling at her quizzically. 'Couldn't you bring yourself to say "Marcus", Julia? Just for once? I rather fancy the others might find it odd, otherwise.'

'Whatever you say. You're the boss,' she said cheerfully, and examined her surroundings with an interest Marcus watched indulgently.

'Have you never been here before, Julia?'

'No. A bit above my touch.'

He frowned. 'Surely you dine out occasionally?'

'Not much.' And certainly not in places as expensive as the Chesterton, she thought, amused, and changed the subject to the age and former role of the building, which had once been the house of a local nobleman in the days when the spa was visited by Royalty to drink the waters.

Marcus grimaced. 'Vile stuff. Have you ever tasted it?'

Julia shook her head. 'I don't intend to, either.'

'Have another of these instead.'

'I'd better not—I'd prefer to keep as sober as possible. I have a function to perform tonight, remember.'

Marcus brushed her hand lightly with his long, slim fingers. 'I'd like to think you enjoyed the evening at the same time, Julia.'

'Oh, I will,' she assured him, trying to hide the fact that his touch had a distinctly electrifying effect. 'But I can do that just as well with a clear head.'

'You know,' said Marcus huskily, 'I have an ambition to see you just slightly *less* clear-headed some time. Are you always so cool and collected, Julia? Doesn't anything ever ruffle you?' His eyes looked almost black in the subdued lighting as they held hers, and Julia stared back, mesmerised, suddenly unable to breathe, and he leaned towards her involuntarily, then halted, cursing softly under his breath, and the spell was broken.

Julia felt slightly dazed as she turned to see a couple in the doorway, waving as Marcus sprang to his feet. She followed suit more slowly as a broad-shouldered man in a white dinner jacket pumped Marcus by the hand and a tall, slender woman in a beaded black dress reached up to kiss Marcus on both cheeks.

Marcus turned to bring Julia forward. 'Let me introduce you to Julia North, who organises my business life efficiently and kindly spares the time to do so in the evening occasionally.'

'Glad to know you, Julia! Dwight McAllister,' said the burly, sandy-haired man, shaking her enthusiastically by the hand. 'This is my new bride, Nancy.'

The couple looked very prosperous and healthy and energetic to Julia, as she shook hands and said all the appropriate things expected, asking how Nancy McAllister liked the town, and whether she knew the UK well.

'This is my first time, Julia. I'd never even been out of the States until I met Dwight. Now I'm getting to be a regular little globe-trotter.' Nancy exchanged a glance with her husband. 'He spoils me.'

The mutual look between husband and wife was so full of warmth and love Julia felt a slight thickening in her throat before the waiter arrived with drinks, but the moment passed as Marcus set out to be the entertaining host Julia had fully expected him to be. The four of them had been chatting easily for the best part of half an hour, until she began to wonder if the chef was likely to tear his hair if they were late starting dinner, before Garrett Lang hurried in, holding his breathless wife by the hand as he embarked on a flood of apologies.

'Stop, stop!' said Marcus, laughing. 'It's those hell-born delinquents of yours. Don't even bother to explain.'

'They let the puppy get at Garrett's black shoes,' said Claire Lang in a rush. 'Please forgive us, everyone. Hello, Nancy, Dwight—lovely to see you again.' She turned to Julia with a warm smile on her rather long but very attractive face. 'And you must be Mrs North, Miss Pennycook's successor. I've been dying to meet you.'

'We were convinced Marcus would never find anyone to take Cookie's place,' said Garrett, grinning. 'But he's come up covered with violets, as usual. Mrs North is just as efficient, half the age and twice as pretty.'

'Garrett Lang!' remonstrated Nancy. 'You're making the girl blush!'

Dwight McAllister's broad smile was teasing. 'Pity she's married, Marcus, old buddy!'

Julia smiled back. 'I'm not married—now, Mr McAllister. I'm a widow, and have been for several years,' she added hastily at the consternation on the Americans' faces. Claire Lang, she could see, already knew. She excused herself and went quickly to the foyer, where the head waiter was hovering with menus, and told him they were ready to order.

In the hubbub of consultation over choices Marcus said in an undertone, 'All right, Julia?'

She smiled at him. 'Perfectly—Marcus.'

His answering smile bathed her in a warm glow which stayed with her as the six of them went up to the private room reserved for dinner in an atmosphere of relaxed conviviality Julia found very much to her taste. She was seated at a round table between Dwight McAllister and Garrett Lang. Both men were attentive and so easy to talk to that any initial fears she might have had about her ability to hold her own in the lively general conversation soon disappeared. And since a five-course meal never normally featured in her life Julia ate very sparingly of the chilled avocado soup and lobster soufflé which followed it, determined to enjoy the main course, and everything else put in front of her. As she ate she noted how Marcus paid equal attention to both Nancy McAllister and his sister-in-law, and cast glances across the table now and then to make sure all was well with herself, which rather touched Julia. She began on her *tournedos en croûte*, wondering just exactly why her own presence had been necessary to him at all tonight. Garrett and Claire were family, the McAllisters were obviously old friends; it seemed odd that anyone as self-sufficient as Marcus Lang could feel he needed a female partner for what was, after all, a purely social occasion.

When the meal was over Julia discreetly shepherded the ladies to a bathroom reserved for their use, but Nancy McAllister, who was staying in the hotel, elected to go up to her room to replace a laddered stocking, leaving the other two alone together.

'You live right here in the town, Julia?' asked Claire, touching up her lipstick.

'Yes. Near enough to walk to work.'

'And how do you like working for Marcus?'

'Very much.'

Claire smiled at her warmly. 'You must come out to our place. Perhaps you know it—we live in a converted farmhouse about a couple of miles from Marcus's house.'

'No, I don't know it,' said Julia, longing for escape. 'I've never been to Mr Lang's house.'

'Of course, you haven't been with him long—silly of me. Anyway, you're welcome to come out to Rigg Farm any time you like. Meet my two horrors, if you're brave enough.'

Julia felt wretched. None of this was part of her plan. The idea was to make Garrett suffer, Claire too, not fall victim to their charm. It seemed traitorous to like them both so much. If only it were possible to respond to the spontaneous warmth in Claire's invitation, she thought with sudden longing. It would be wonderful to take Sam to a farm to play.... She clamped down on her traitorous thoughts and smiled at Claire, who was watching her with rather puzzled blue eyes.

'That's very kind of you, Mrs Lang,' she said hurriedly. 'Perhaps I will one day.'

'Oh, Claire, please, Julia!'

Julia was glad when it was time to rejoin the men, who were waiting with brandy and liqueurs for the ladies' return. As Julia began to pour coffee Nancy McAllister arrived, full of apologies, and the conversation soon took on the comfortable, bantering tone of people who were full of good food and happy in each other's company. With the removal of the dinner table the company had regrouped. Julia found Marcus by her side, ready to hand round cups and pour brandy, and afterwards he sat beside her as naturally as though they had hosted dozens of other dinners together.

'You're enjoying the evening, Julia?' he asked under cover of the others' conversation.

'Very much. I'm not perfectly sure why I'm here, but I hope I'm fulfilling whatever function you've brought me here to perform,' she said quietly.

'To the letter.' He gave her a very straight look, then turned away in answer to a sally from the cigar-smoking Dwight, who was chaffing Marcus about the latest addition to Lang Holdings. Nancy promptly banned all business talk and launched into a description of the plays Dwight had taken her to in the West End, which was followed by an account of the latest horror story about Charlie and David Lang from their doting parents. Julia parried any good-natured questions about her own life with an ease born of long practice, and if sometimes Marcus or Claire's eyes narrowed a little, no one else seemed to realise that little more was known about Julia North at the end of the evening than at the beginning.

When the party broke up Julia was exhausted. It was hard to keep on her guard all the time, to be unforth-coming about herself without being unfriendly or even downright rude. She was also dismayed by how much she liked Claire Lang. And by how very plain it was that Garrett and Claire were still very much in love after several years of marriage.

'You look tired,' said Marcus, as they waited in the foyer later for a taxi.

'I am a little,' admitted Julia, and smiled. 'But only enjoyably so. It's been a lovely evening.'

'Yes,' agreed Marcus softly. 'The best evening I've had for some time. Thank you for making it all run so smoothly.'

'I did very little.'

'On the contrary, Julia. You were the best of hostesses: unobtrusive, attentive, a good listener.' By this time the foyer was deserted, and there was no one to see as he took her hand in his. 'Will you do the same again when necessary?'

Julia swallowed nervously, deeply conscious of their clasped hands. 'Yes.'

'And would you still say yes if I asked you to dine with just me for company?' he asked huskily, and moved closer. She stiffened, and moved away a little.

'I'm not sure that would be wise.'

'Why?' he demanded. 'Because you're my secretary, you mean?'

'Yes.' And because I just might get to like you too much, thought Julia with regret, and where would that get me, for heaven's sake?

'You mean I shouldn't try to mix business with pleasure,' Marcus said wryly. 'Not that I'm in the habit of wining and dining my secretary, I assure you.'

Julia laughed a little, involuntarily. 'I don't suppose Miss Pennycook would have allowed it!'

Marcus laughed with her, then eyed her curiously. 'By the way, Julia, just exactly what is there about Claire that you find so riveting, I wonder? Several times this evening I surprised you looking at her in a very odd way.'

Julia removed her hand from his abruptly. 'Not odd, Mr Lang. Just interested. She's a very charming lady.'

'Ah! The party's over. I've reverted to Mr Lang again.' His tone was dry, but to Julia's relief he seemed diverted from the subject of Claire, and the arrival of the taxi made it possible to avoid any further reference to her on the way home.

She was surprised to find Marcus intended sharing the taxi.

'I left the Ferrari in the hotel car park,' he said as he sat beside her in the back of the car. 'Where do you live?'

With great reluctance Julia told him, fully aware that he was unlikely to let her get out in Chester Square and walk the rest of the way unescorted at that time of night. And to the detriment of her self-possession Marcus took her hand again and refused to release it when she made a half-hearted attempt to pull away. Julia hardly knew whether to be glad or sorry when the taxi drew up at her front gate and he helped her out, then walked with her to her front door, and out of earshot of the taxi driver.

She offered him her hand formally.

'Thank you for a lovely evening.' She flicked a hand at her dress. 'And for everything else. I just wish I knew why you felt my presence was necessary.'

Marcus laughed in the summer darkness. 'I thought tonight would be a fairly easy preparation for the next time, when it's likely to be six hard-bitten businessmen with elderly wives who want to talk about their grand-children, or electronic engineers who spend the entire evening babbling in jargon.'

Both of which would be a lot easier in some ways, thought Julia. She tried to pull away, but his slim, hard hand tightened on hers as he drew her towards him and bent to kiss her once, very gently, on the cheek.

'Goodnight, Julia. Sleep well.'

'Goodnight,' she said unsteadily, and he touched a hand to the place he'd just kissed and turned to go.

Julia watched his tall figure retreat down the path, then let herself quietly into the dark house.

'Well?' whispered Laura, yawning, as she wandered into the narrow hall. 'How did it go?'

'Very well—but you shouldn't be down here. Sam would have been all right on his own.'

'He sounded a bit restless, so I thought I'd bring a book down here and wait to see how you got on.'

Julia took off her shoes and tiptoed into Sam's room, where a nightlight cast a faint glow on the flushed, sleeping face. She hung over him for a while, then went into the kitchen where Laura was switching on the kettle for tea.

'He seems peaceful enough now.'

'He was probably tuned in to your nervous tension earlier on.' Laura thrust a cup of tea towards her. 'Now tell me all about it.'

And Julia did, giving a detailed account of the food and the guests and the conversation, and the dresses of the other two women.

'And what did you think of Claire Lang?' asked Laura quietly.

Julia sighed, and unfastened the pearl clip to run her fingers through her hair. 'Ironic, isn't it? I like her—I like her a lot. And the more I get to know Garrett, the more I like him too.'

Laura shook her head, smiling fondly. 'Frankly, Julia North, if you want my opinion, you're an absolute washout in the role of Nemesis!'

CHAPTER FIVE

JULIA had been employed at Lang Holdings for almost five months when she came to a decision she knew had been inevitable ever since the night of the dinner-party at the Chesterton Hotel. Somehow she had managed to keep her relationship with Marcus from becoming too involved, but it had been uphill work in the face of his obvious intention to put matters on a far more personal basis. Subtly and steadily he had built on the advantage gained that night, without ever encroaching so much that Julia could object. Not that she wanted to object. The more she grew to know Marcus Lang, the more she re-alised how easy it would be to make their relationship as personal as it was possible to be. If only... But that was the point where she always put her mental brakes on and reminded herself that any relationship, other than professional, with Marcus was out of the question. And Christmas was almost upon them, Sam's third already, she realised with a pang. It was high time to act on her decision, before she lost the will to act on it at all.

'Good lord, Julia, that's a ferocious expression!' said Marcus, as he swept into her office the day before Christmas Eve.

'Good morning.' Julia smiled at him. 'I was going over my shopping list, wondering if I'd forgotten anything.'

'Everything organised for the dance tonight?'

She nodded. 'Yes. Claire says the wine and beer has arrived at Rigg Farm and the caterers are due there later this afternoon. I gather she's threatened to cancel Christmas if Charlie and David commit even the tiniest of crimes.'

Marcus shook his head, grinning, as he divested himself of his overcoat. 'Claire's an optimist. Short of chaining them up, I don't quite know how she's going to manage that.'

'I think she's an angel to have the office party at her home in the first place,' said Julia, pouring him a cup of coffee.

Marcus downed it almost in one gulp. 'Thanks, I needed that. It's bloody cold out there today.' He eyed her challengingly. 'But then you just think Claire's an angel, period, don't you?'

Julia flushed. 'She's a warm, friendly lady.'

'And wonders all the time why you refuse to visit her. Why won't you?' he shot at her suddenly.

'I've been very busy,' said Julia evasively, and glanced pointedly at her watch. 'Do you think we could make a start? I've promised to meet someone for lunch today.'

'Who?'

She raised an eyebrow. 'Sue Rivers.'

'Sue Rivers? Who's she?' he demanded.

'One of your typists,' said Julia patiently, 'and now and then we have lunch together.'

'But I wanted you to have lunch with me today,' he said irritably.

She blinked. This was new. She had dined with Marcus several times since that first dinner-party, but always as hostess to a group of businessmen and their wives. Not once had Marcus proposed a meal *à deux* again.

'I always took Miss Pennycook to lunch at Christmas time,' said Marcus slyly, 'so no one would cast a stone at my impeccable Mrs North if she were seen lunching with her employer, you know.'

'Sorry,' said Julia lightly. 'I promised Sue.'

'Then you'll just have to promise to dance with me a lot tonight by way of reparation.'

She eyed him suspiciously, and he laughed at her.

'Just getting into the festive spirit, Julia. Nothing to worry about.'

She smiled wryly, then followed him into his office with her notebook and got on with the day's routine as she always did.

'What are you wearing tonight, Julia?' asked Sue eagerly, over toasted sandwiches and a shared pot of tea in their usual haunt.

'Something warm, I should think. The barn at Rigg Farm is likely to be draughty.' Julia smiled warmly at the younger girl. Sue was staying overnight in the town with her fiancé's family. On her left hand she proudly wore the new engagement ring her Philip had bought her only a week or two before, and she was obviously looking forward to showing him off in front of her friends. She sighed blissfully.

'I'm so looking forward to tonight. The Lang Christmas dances are always a tremendous success. Mr Lang thinks up something different every year—though I've only been to one so far myself, of course. And that was at the Village Hall near Mr Lang's house.'

'I can't think why Claire Lang's letting herself in for this shindig tonight,' said Julia, shaking her head.

'But I expect *you*'ve done all the organising,' said Sue loyally.

'That was the easy part. The Langs get all the mess and bother, not to mention keeping their boys out of mischief.'

'They're smashing little boys, though,' chuckled Sue. 'Have you seen them?'

'Yes. Double trouble personified.' Julia got up. 'Must run, Sue—I've got a bit of shopping to get in before I go home.'

'It's lovely to have the afternoon off, isn't it?' Sue reached happily for another cake. 'See you tonight.'

Julia smiled indulgently. 'See you, Sue.'

She hurried through her shopping and walked rapidly home through the bright, cold afternoon. Shoppers were out in full force, and she was glad to leave the crowded pavements of the city centre for the quiet of the roads in her own part of town. She turned down into Chester Road, to see Laura approaching in the opposite direction with Daisy by the hand and Sam in the pushchair. As he saw Julia he let out a roar, and Laura released him from his harness so he could run towards Julia, who waited, arms outstretched as Sam hurled himself into them, losing his red woolly hat and one of his mittens in the process.

'Mummy!' he shrieked, beaming. 'You home!'

Julia hugged him, rubbing her cold cheek against his rosy one. 'Yes, I'm home, Sam. Have you been a good boy?'

He nodded solemnly as she set him on his feet. 'Sam good boy.'

'Is he telling the truth, Daisy, love?' asked Julia, and the little girl giggled.

'*Quite* good, Auntie Julia.'

Laura let her daughter take charge of the empty push-chair as Julia took Sam by the hand for the short walk to the house. 'All set for the do tonight, Julia?'

'I suppose so.' Julia made a face. 'I hate the thought of it.'

'Why?'

'To me the words "office party" are synonymous with trouble, as you well know.'

Laura unlocked their communal front door, looking over her shoulder at Julia. 'I do. Is tonight the night, by any chance? Are you finally going to let the sword of Damocles down on the heads of the clan Lang?'

'It's the ideal opportunity, certainly.' Julia began divesting Sam of his windcheater in the warmth of the kitchen.

Laura put a pan of milk to warm on the Aga. 'Let's have some hot chocolate and unwind—only put that fascinating bag of goodies somewhere before Sam manages to unwrap anything.'

'Oh, lord!' Julia flew to rescue the bag, and went off to hide it in her bedroom, then went back to spend a relaxing, pleasant hour with Laura while the children sat, rapt, in front of a Disney cartoon film.

Later on, to Sam's intense delight, it began to snow, and he bounced up and down at the window, watching the flakes, demanding to go outside to catch them, but Julia shook her head firmly.

'Tomorrow we'll go out in it, Sam. It's too late now. Let's play with your blocks instead.'

Reluctantly Sam let himself be diverted, and soon afterwards Laura went up to her own flat to prepare dinner, leaving her little daughter downstairs with the others until bathtime. The children played quite happily for a time, and Julia just sat watching them, her mind on the evening ahead. Perhaps fate would intervene, and it would snow enough to make it impossible to get out to Rigg Farm. But Marcus owned a Range Rover, so he'd just send someone to fetch her, which washed that out. Julia curled up in her chair, feeling drowsy in the warmth, her eyes heavy as they rested on the two small figures sitting cross-legged, their concentration intense as they balanced one block on another in a perilous structure which eventually toppled over to the accompaniment of angry roars from Sam and giggles from Daisy.

A shiny red apple each gave the construction engineers encouragement to start over again, while Julia wrestled with the problem confronting her. Tonight had always been the occasion designated in her mind for the climax of her plan. She had been working for it ever since the day she began changing herself from an ordinary girl who taught nursery school into the superefficient secretary who had managed to get the job she had coveted at Lang's. And now the time had come. The final hurdle was here, and she hated the very thought of it. Then her hazel eyes fell on Sam's profile, and hardened. It was for his sake, she reminded herself, not her own. She couldn't allow herself even to consider wasting all the hard work and sacrifice which had led up to tonight. The confrontation ahead was one she had rehearsed so many times mentally that it would probably go like clockwork once she took the plunge.

Later, dressed in a heavy wool skirt that swirled about her ankles, and a fine wool shirt in the same shade of rich dark red, Julia sprayed herself with perfume, threaded her mother's pearl drops into her ear-lobes, fastened the little pearl pin to her collar, and pulled on the glove-thin black leather boots she felt were most suitable for a barn-dance. She looked in at the sleeping Sam, who lay on his back, arms outflung as usual, his hair dark against the pillow. It was no longer such a wrench for her to leave him in the evening. Since she had started working for Marcus, evenings out were a more regular occurrence, and Sam had grown used to having Laura on hand now and then if he woke.

Julia drew the quilt higher over the sleeping child, switched on the intercom, then went up to Laura to say she was about to leave. Tristan Murray answered her knock, and whistled in admiration at the sight of her.

'All ready for the Christmas jolly, I see, Mrs North.' His teeth glinted wickedly in his luxuriant red beard. His appearance was arresting, as usual; bright green wool shirt spattered with paint, and a pair of dungarees that had seen better days. He pulled at the gold ring in his ear, ogling Julia, then called to his wife. 'Sweetheart, our seductive landlady is ready for the off. Come and see—she looks quite edible!'

'Don't mind him,' said Laura, and thrust a large bin-bag full of wrapping paper and mysterious objects at her husband. 'Just take that downstairs to Julia's sitting-room and stop drooling, you lecher.' She smiled approvingly at Julia. 'Perfect for the occasion, love—one way and another.'

Julia coloured. 'I'd better go—but why are you coming downstairs? Sam will be fine with the intercom.'

'We thought we'd listen for Daisy tonight instead, and pack parcels in your place to avoid the chance of our daughter wandering in to see what's going on.' Laura gave her a little push, her silver bracelets tinkling. 'Go on, Daughter of the Night—get it over with.'

Tris looked at his wife, mystified. 'Why all the veiled allusions, my angel? Something you're keeping from me?'

'No,' said Julia. 'Something *I'm* keeping from you. But Laura can break her vow of silence now. You'd have known tomorrow, anyway.' She smiled bleakly. 'I'm likely to need a cork shoulder, so be warned!'

The doorbell rang, and Julia bade the others a hasty farewell, flew to see if Sam had woken up, then, re-assured, collected her coat on the way to open the door to the taxi-driver. She stared in astonishment at the tall figure of Marcus Lang.

'Hello, Julia. I cancelled your cab. It's snowing a bit, so I thought I'd fetch you in the Range Rover.' He grinned down at her astonished face, then Julia recollected herself hurriedly, smiling politely as she closed the door behind her and went with him down the path.

'That's very kind of you,' she said with a sinking heart. Her task was plainly not going to be made easier for her. 'But quite unnecessary. The snow's not sticking.'

'I know.' Marcus tossed her up into the high front seat, then hurried round to get in his own side. 'Brr! It's damned unpleasant out there just the same. I can see half the merrymakers sleeping in Garrett's barn if this keeps up.'

How expensive the aura of this man was, thought Julia, as she glanced up at the profile she now knew so well. He exuded good soap and expensive cloth, mingled with the leather of the upholstery, and a faint tang of the cigars he occasionally smoked. But no alcohol, she noted in approval. But of course, Marcus Lang never endangered his professional reputation in any way.

Losing his driving licence for the sake of a drink or two was hardly his style.

'You're very quiet,' he commented, as they left town in the direction of Rigg Farm.

'Just surprised.'

'To see me, you mean?'

It was too dark in the vehicle's interior to see his face, but his voice sounded amused. Julia wondered if the boredom was in his eyes as usual, then frowned, struck by something she had only subconsciously noted over the past month or two. The boredom which had been so prevalent in Marcus's expression at first rarely appeared in his eyes these days. If she had thought more about him, instead of Garrett, she would have realised that Marcus was rather more human now than when she first began to work for him.

'Well?'

Julia flushed in the darkness, and thanked him for being so considerate—rather belatedly, she realised, embarrassed.

'I came to fetch you because I wanted a few words in private, before we get to the party,' Marcus informed her. 'These affairs can get rowdy, you know. So beware of amorous overtures from stray Lotharios made bold by drink and the odd lack of licence they seem to think an office party allows.'

'I don't expect any overtures will be made to *me*!' said Julia.

'Why not?'

'Did Miss Pennycook have any trouble?'

Marcus laughed. 'No, I can't say she did.'

'Then why should I? I hold down the same job.'

'Exceedingly well too.' He reached out a hand and touched hers fleetingly. 'But the similarity ends there, Julia. You're half Miss Pennycook's age, and a very good-looking lady. And don't imagine that touch-me-not manner of yours is a put-off, either. Most men probably regard it as a challenge.'

Julia's jaw dropped. 'You're not serious!'

'I am, you know. Heaven knows it challenges *me*, so I assume it has the same effect on most other men. Apart from Garrett, probably.'

'How interesting,' said Julia tartly. 'Am I allowed to ask why your brother should be immune?'

'Because, without descending to sheer schmaltz, Garrett has never had eyes for anyone but Claire since the first day they met in college.' Marcus chuckled as they turned on to a narrow minor road. 'We all lived at home then, and the family had to put up with his extravagant outpourings about Claire. We expected to loathe her on sight.'

'But you didn't, of course,' said Julia absently, trying to digest yet another unknown facet of Garrett Lang's personality. 'Funny, really—he seems so outgoing and—and gregarious, I would have pictured him flitting from one girl to another when he was younger.'

'He did before he met Claire. Then his entire energy was taken up trying to disabuse her of the same idea as you.'

Julia suddenly noticed the car was slowing as Marcus turned into a farm gateway to park. 'Why have we stopped?' she asked quickly.

'Because I wanted to give you your Christmas present now,' said Marcus casually, apparently unaware of his companion's utter dismay.

It had been Julia's task to purchase impersonal gifts of perfume for the Lang female staff en masse, and she had taken it for granted that her own gift was likely to be similar, possibly chosen by Claire Lang. Marcus switched on the interior light of the Range Rover and handed her a narrow, gift-wrapped package. Julia took it gingerly, staring down at it in something almost like anguish. This was unbearable. She hadn't even anticipated a gift handed over by Marcus personally.

'Go on,' said the hard voice gently. 'Open it. It won't bite.'

With unsteady fingers she removed the gilt paper from a long leather jewel-box, and stared wide-eyed at the string of pearls on a bed of white satin inside. Oh, no, she thought in dread. It's not fair!

'I never see you wear any jewellery other than the earrings you have on now, and a little brooch something the same, so as it seemed you like pearls I thought these would please you.'

Julia could hear a questioning note in Marcus's voice and cleared her throat. 'They're lovely—quite lovely. But far too much.' How could she tell him that to her the creamy pearls looked exactly like coals of fire?

'Nonsense! You work yourself very hard for me, Julia North. These are a mere token of my appreciation,' he said matter-of-factly, and took the pearls from their box. 'Here, bend your head forward. I'll fasten them for you.'

Julia did as he asked, biting her lip hard when his fingers touched the nape of her neck as he fastened the clasp.

'You can sit up again now,' he said gently, and she raised her head, turning to look up into the watchful eyes which looked dark tonight, and far too intuitive for her peace of mind.

'Thank you,' she managed huskily at last. 'But you really——'

'Now don't start telling me what I can or can't do,' he said lightly. 'If you're worried about any hint of propriety, no one knows I've given you anything, not even Garrett or Claire. And most women own a string of pearls of some kind.'

'But these are real pearls!'

'So are the ones you wear in your ears. Besides,' he added softly, holding her eyes, 'I don't care for fakes.'

Julia went cold, unable to tear her eyes away. What did he mean? Did he guess?

To her dismay Marcus misinterpreted her inability to look away, and bent his head and kissed her lightly. He raised his head very slightly to stare into her astonished eyes, then slid a hand behind her head and kissed her again, anything but lightly. Julia tried to break free, but he slid an arm about her and pulled her close, reaching up the other hand to turn off the light, and to her indignation went on kissing her with mounting enthusiasm. Since she was wearing a fur-lined jacket and so was he she was conscious of nothing beyond the simple contact of their bodies and the hard warmth of the lips which refused to release her own. She began to tremble at the realisation that she liked being kissed. It had been so long since a man had held her and kissed her and made her conscious of her own femininity that she forgot that this was her employer, no mere ordinary male. Then dimly she realised that Marcus Lang was no mere ordinary male anyway. He was as skilled at his present occupation as he was at running a successful business empire, and she wanted to surrender herself into his keeping and have him hold her and keep her safe and warm like this indefinitely.

The last conclusion was enough to make herself jerk away, breathing hard, furious with herself. What on earth did she imagine she was doing! Getting fond of Marcus Lang was no part of her plan. And after tonight he was highly unlikely to want to set eyes on her again, let alone give her pearls and kiss her and make her feel so—so *wanted*.

'I apologise, Julia,' he said unevenly. 'I had no idea—I mean, I never intended——'

It was so flattering to hear him sound like a stammering schoolboy that Julia cooled down quickly. 'Please don't worry. I quite understand. The past minute or two never happened as far as I'm concerned.'

There was silence for or moment.

'It was almost fifteen minutes, to be precise,' he informed her, with a note in his voice she hadn't heard for some time. The boredom appeared to be back.

'In that case,' said Julia briskly, 'we're late. Would you mind driving on?' She reached up trembling fingers to take off the pearls. 'And I really can't accept such an expensive present.'

'If you imagine I was after your body in exchange,' he said, starting the car, 'you're wrong. So for goodness' sake keep the pearls. Otherwise I'll throw them in the ditch. Sell the bloody things if your principles are offended by them.'

Since Julia found she couldn't undo the clasp, she was obliged to do as he said. It seemed unwise to risk the touch of his fingers on her neck again, even less wise to ask him to stop the car so that he could remove the necklace. As the Range Rover crunched back on to the road again she felt utterly depressed. What a start to the evening! And from her own point of view, at least, if not from the merrymaking employees of Lang's already gathered at Rigg Farm, the wretched evening could only go downhill. And what was more, to carry out her plan she would have to wait until all the rest had gone home before she could put it into operation.

The brief journey passed in silence, and Julia was heartily glad when Rigg Farm came into view, lights blazing from every window, music coming from the barn. A large conifer stood nearby, hung with Christmas lights in a way that ordinarily would have gladdened her heart. As it was her heart sank even further as she thought of the hours ahead during which she'd be obliged to dance and laugh and contribute her two cents' worth of Christmas cheer to the festivities.

Claire and Garrett appeared in the doorway, the former in a bright blue skirt, the latter in jeans, both of them in identical checked wool shirts and looking far too young to be the parents of the two small boys they held by the hand.

'For Pete's sake come and say goodnight to these two villains,' Garrett implored. 'They refuse to go to bed until you take them up personally.'

Marcus laughed, any coolness between himself and Julia going unnoticed in the storm of protest from Charlie and David as their uncle bore them off into the house, leaving Garrett and Claire to usher Julia into the barn, which was the scene of much thumping and stamping as a caller yelled the moves of a barn-dance, and all the employees of Lang's, plus wives, sweethearts, husbands, and others of categories not so well defined, swung their partners with wild skirling shrieks.

'Wow!' said Julia, impressed. 'Have they been doing this long?'

'Long enough,' grinned Garrett. 'Come and have a drink, while I take your coat.'

'You look terrific,' said Claire, as she took Julia to the bar set up in one corner. 'What'll you have? Wine?'

'Yes, please. Anything.' Julia gazed at the whooping, whirling crowd wide-eyed. 'My goodness, everyone's having such a fantastic time!'

'Congratulate Claire,' said Garrett, joining them. 'It was her idea. She did the decorations too.'

The building was a bower of holly and mistletoe and trailing ivy, with clusters of gold bells and shiny red apples at intervals, and miniature Christmas trees on the small tables lining the walls.

'It's beautiful, Claire,' said Julia with sincerity. 'How hard you must have worked!'

Garrett clasped his wife's shoulders tenderly. 'And never a word of complaint, either, in spite of those aching muscles!'

'I'm not aching now,' Claire protested. 'Besides, it was a wonderful way to keep Charlie and David occupied now they've finished school for the holidays. They've been at it all day, working like beavers, channelling their energies very successfully, thank heavens.'

The dance came to an end and the dancers sifted back to the tables while the musicians put down their fiddles and banjos and picked up guitars, the caller taking his place at the drums.

'Music for the youngsters now,' said Garrett. 'Let's repair to our table to wait for Marcus. With my usual matchless forethought I remembered to put a reserved sign on one in a corner, farthest away from the band.'

To Julia's dismay she found she was expected to share a table with only the other three, all the other members of management distributed round the room among their staff. She felt as though all eyes were turned in their direction as Marcus reappeared and made his way towards them, stopping here and there to greet various members of the workforce and submit to introductions where necessary, renewing acquaintance with relatives met previously.

'Right,' he said with a sigh as he took the fourth chair at the table. 'The boys are in bed. Mrs Bray has permission to use physical violence if they try to steal past her to get back here, and I've done the required social niceties, so perhaps now I can relax a bit.'

How fortunate that he was able to, thought Julia with resentment. She found it quite impossible to relax. The episode in the car had totally wrecked what little peace of mind she'd had in the first place tonight. She stole a glance at Marcus, to find him watching her. He raised his glass of beer in toast.

'Cheers, Julia. Here's to your first Christmas with Lang's.'

'Amen to that,' said Garrett cheerfully, then winced as the band crashed into the latest chart-topper. 'Come on, Claire, let's get on the floor. Must set a good example.'

They left Julia and Marcus at the table in what would have been an awkward silence if the music hadn't been belting through the raftered building as the floor filled with energetic dancers. The tables nearest them were deserted, and after a while Marcus moved his chair closer to Julia so that he could speak directly into her ear.

'I'm sorry, Julia, I'm afraid I spoiled your evening before it even began.'

She looked up at him, into eyes which appeared almost black tonight under the shifting strobe lights which cast different colours round the stone walls. 'No, you didn't do that. I know the—the kiss was unintentional. I'm sure the pearls are just what you said—a token of appreciation.'

'Then why are you so subdued, Julia?' He moved closer. 'What's troubling you?'

Julia thought rapidly. 'It's—just that Christmas tends to be a painful time for me, that's all.'

'Is that when your husband died?'

'Not exactly. But it's the time of year that makes memories poignant, I suppose.'

Marcus eyed her downcast face thoughtfully as the music changed, slowing to a less frenetic beat. 'Will you dance with me, Julia? I think I can manage whatever it is one does to this.'

She nodded and rose to her feet, but with a reluctance he plainly found amusing, as she let him hold her close in keeping with the slow tempo as they mingled with the crowd. Julia looked steadfastly over Marcus's shoulder as they moved together, seeing faces she saw every day, some of them curious, some of them smiling. Sue's round rapt face was pressed close to the cheek of a fair-haired youth who was obviously her Philip, and Rowena, one of the receptionists, went by in the arms of one of the marketing men. But it was hard to keep herself erect and unyielding in Marcus Lang's arms, Julia found. Since he was a head taller than herself she found her cheek brushing his shoulder however much she tried to avoid contact. And he looked so different tonight in a black and red chequered shirt with black cord trousers and a black suede waistcoat, in keeping with the general mood of the festivities. He looked younger, and almost alarmingly attractive. Probably, Julia told herself severely, because she normally never saw him dressed other than in expensive suits or formal dinner jacket.

'We blend well together, don't you think?' he murmured in her ear, and she looked up at him, frowning. 'Colour scheme,' he said helpfully. 'People will think we planned it beforehand.'

Julia's cheeks flamed to tone in with her shirt, and she dropped her eyes, turning her head away. 'I certainly hope not,' she said tartly.

'Are you worried about your reputation?' he asked drily.

'No.' Which was true enough. After tonight, her reputation would be the least of her concerns.

Suddenly the music changed, and the master of ceremonies called for everyone to take their places for an eightsome reel, and at once Garrett and Claire dashed to their side with four other people in tow, and for a time Julia forgot everything in remembering the movements of the dance, laughing helplessly when she got it wrong at first, then loving the fun of it all as the dancers grew more expert and went through the figures without a hitch, calling for an encore afterwards so they could repeat the performance.

The evening went on with a change of mood every half-hour, a delicious supper eaten at one stage, and afterwards, as a grand finale, a good old-fashioned Paul Jones during the course of which Julia danced with a lot of men she normally met only in a purely business capacity. It was great fun, and an inspiration as a Christmas party, with none of the huddling in dark corners she had thought of as synonymous with this type of occasion. She said as much to Claire at one stage.

'The trick is to keep everyone moving as energetically as possible so that kind of thing just doesn't happen. Just like Charlie and David. The energies must be channelled!' Claire laughed, then jumped up to dance with Marcus to a very conventional foxtrot, as Garrett beckoned Julia on to the floor.

'Enjoyed yourself, Julia?' asked Garrett.

'It's been such fun,' she said sincerely. 'The best evening I've had for ages.'

'I'm glad.' Garrett held her loosely, a little away from him so he could look down at her with the familiar, changeable Lang eyes. 'I thought you looked a bit tense when you first arrived.'

'Nerves. I don't go out very much these days.'

'Because you're a widow?'

'Partly.' Julia could hardly mention Sam, who was the other big reason. That could come later, when all the others had gone. Her face shadowed, and Garrett's smiled coaxingly.

'Now don't get all self-contained again, Mrs North. You've let your hair down very satisfactorily tonight. Keep up the good work!'

She smiled brightly. 'Of course.'

The rhythm changed, and Garrett looked up quickly, his eyes searching out his wife's fair head. 'Would you mind, Julia? This is the last waltz. Shall we change partners?'

Without a word Julia moved into Marcus's arms as
Garrett folded his wife into a close embrace, his eyes
half closed as he leaned his cheek against her hair.

'Do you object to the switch?' said Marcus in her ear.

Julia shook her head, feeling suddenly tired, unable
to keep herself at a distance as he exerted a gentle
pressure on the back of her waist. She let herself lean
against his shoulder, uncaring now whether they were
observed or not. The lights were turned down low, and
in any case, after tonight it wouldn't matter any more.

Afterwards Julia stood with Marcus and Garrett and
Claire as everyone expressed thanks and bade them
goodnight before dispersing to the coaches and taxis
waiting for them. When everyone had gone Claire gave
a great yawn and held out her hand to her husband.

'Let's go up to the house and drink lots and lots of
tea, darling. Come on, Julia. You've hardly drunk a
thing all night.'

Against her will Julia let herself be persuaded. After
all, what did it matter where she exploded her bomb-
shell, here in the barn or inside Garrett Lang's house?
The effect would be the same.

In the huge, warm kitchen, which retained the stone
flags of its original use, the four of them sat round a
scrubbed table and drank tea and coffee according to
preference. Julia was glad of the hot drink. Her whole
body felt like ice now that the moment of truth was finally at hand.

After a while, during which she chatted away with the
others about the evening, both Claire and Garrett excused themselves to take a look at their sons, and Marcus
was left alone with a very weary-looking girl whose
cheeks matched the pearls at her throat.

'What is it, Julia?' he asked gently. 'Are you still upset about the incident in the car? Don't be. It won't be repeated against your wishes, I promise.'

Colour rose in her face and receded, leaving it paler than before. 'No, it's not that.'

'Then what's tuning you to concert pitch, girl? Something's on your mind!'

Julia turned rather desperate eyes on his watchful face. 'When the others come back I have something to say.'

'Something important, obviously.' Marcus frowned, and thrust a hand through his hair. 'Couldn't you have said it earlier and got it off your chest so you could enjoy the evening properly?'

She smiled humourlessly. 'I've been waiting quite a while to say it. Another hour or two made no difference.' She swallowed. 'If you'll excuse me for a moment, I'd rather like to go to the bathroom.'

'First on the right up the stairs,' he said, getting to his feet.

Julia left him quickly, shutting herself in the luxuriously appointed bathroom she found. She leaned against the door, her heart thudding, then went to look in the mirror over the basin. The dark rings round the light irises in her eyes looked more pronounced than usual, a sure sign of stress. Her eyes burned in her colourless face, making her hair look Indian-dark. They stared back at her as though asking her if she meant to go through with it.

'But I must,' she whispered to her reflection. 'I can't change my mind just because...' Just because she happened to like Garrett and Claire Lang far more than she would have believed possible. And could like Marcus Lang very much indeed were the situation different. She had suspected the latter for some time, but his kisses tonight had confirmed it beyond all doubt. Despite his rather despotic outlook on some things, his demands and his impatience with anything less than perfection, Julia knew she could fall in love with Marcus Lang unless she were very careful. In fact, she admitted wearily, perhaps it was already too late. Unacknowledged and un-admitted, perhaps she had been in love with him for some time, without even knowing it.

She ran cold water on her hands, then touched them to her white, burning cheeks. She took a deep breath and opened the door very quietly, checking as she saw the couple in the open door of the bedroom opposite. Held close in each other's arms, Garrett and Claire were kissing each other with a passionate, absorbed intensity Julia witnessed with a hot stab of pain.

She moved and they broke apart, Claire flushing as she saw Julia.

'Sorry, Julia.' She exchanged a laughing glance with her impenitent husband. 'Didn't mean to embarrass you.'

Julia was a mass of conflicting emotions as she went downstairs with the other two to join Marcus, who was still at the kitchen table.

'I made another pot of coffee, *and* one of tea,' he said virtuously, 'since I can't have a drink before driving Julia home.'

'Ten out of ten,' said Claire gratefully, sitting down. 'I could drink the sea dry!'

Garrett held a chair for Julia and straddled another, yawning. 'Pretty successful tonight, wouldn't you say?'

'Very. Both as a social event and a public relations exercise.' Marcus raised his mug in solemn toast. 'Now pray silence for Mrs Julia North, who tells me she has something important to announce.'

Three pairs of eyes fixed on Julia's face, and she swallowed drily. So say it, she told herself fiercely. Get on with it. She cleared her throat. 'I—I merely wanted to say how much I enjoy working for Lang's, and—and how much I appreciate the friendliness and hospitality you've all shown me,' she said in a rush, then gulped down the hot tea in her cup, never even noticing when it scalded her throat as it went down.

CHAPTER SIX

THE DRIVE home was undertaken in silence so thick with unspoken questions Julia could have screamed by the time the Range Rover came to a halt outside the house.

'Thank you for a lovely evening, and for bringing me home, and—and for the pearls,' she said, wrestling with the door-handle.

'It's locked,' said Marcus. 'And for pity's sake stop babbling.' He caught her by the arm and turned her towards him. 'I would give much to know what you really meant to say tonight, Julia. Your improvised speech was unconvincing, to say the least.'

Her lashes dropped to hide her eyes.

'Can't you tell *me*?' he persisted gently.

'I said what I meant to say,' she said woodenly. 'Now if you'll excuse me I must go in. It's late.'

He held her a moment longer, then shrugged and released her arm. 'All right, if you won't, you won't. But Julia, please, if you do have a problem I'd be very happy to help solve it. Right from the start I've felt there was some burden you feel you have to carry through life.'

How right he was! Julia would have smiled at the irony of it if she'd had the energy. But right now all she wanted was bed for a few brief hours before Sam had her out of it again.

'There's nothing, really.' The lie lay light on her conscience. The opportunity for truth had come and gone and she'd funked it, and that was that. 'Goodnight, Marcus. Have a happy Christmas.'

'How will you spend Christmas Day, Julia? Are you going away?'

'No. I'm having lunch with friends.'

'Good. I wouldn't like to think of you alone.' Marcus leaned across her to release the catch on the door, then brushed his lips to her hair briefly. Julia sat, numb, as he jumped out of the car and went round to open her door. Marcus held up his arms and she slid down into them, and he held her for a heartbeat before letting her go.

'Goodnight, Julia. See you next week.'

'Yes. Goodnight. And thank you again.'

Marcus stood bareheaded in the falling snow as Julia went up the path and put her key in the lock with trembling fingers. Tears formed on her lashes as she let herself in the house without a backward glance, and after only a cursory look at Sam Julia tore off her clothes, burrowed under the bedclothes and cried herself to sleep.

Next morning she looked a mess. When Sam's peremptory call jerked her out of a brief, heavy sleep she got up feeling worse than she could ever remember feeling, short of being actually ill. She shuddered at the sight of her face in the mirror, pulled on her dressing-gown and went to Sam's room to take him out of bed and dress him, finding the effort of responding cheerfully to his early-morning *joie de vivre* almost beyond her. By the time she'd drunk a pot full of tea, while Sam despatched porridge and a boiled egg, Julia began to feel better. She took him into her bedroom afterwards and let him play with her shoes while she dressed in warm jersey and cord trousers, then hung up the clothes she

had hurled on the floor the night before in her desperate
need to get into bed and blot out the world.

What a failure she was, she thought bleakly, as she
set about tidying the flat with the help and hindrance of
Sam for company as he trailed about after her with a
duster, delighted he was to have her company all day
instead of being handed over to Laura. Later on Tristan
knocked on the sitting-room door and popped his red
head around it.

'I'm taking Daisy off to the park to throw snowballs.
Would Sam like to come too?'

Julia managed a smile. 'Does that mean Laura wants
an account of last night?'

'It certainly does.' He eyed her red, swollen lids with
compassion. 'I also came to offer the cork shoulder, but
I rather fancy the need for that was last night.'

'Very true,' sighed Julia, and called to Sam. 'Do you
want to go to the park with Tris and Daisy, Sam?'

'Snow?' he said hopefully.

'Snow,' agreed Tris. 'And get a move on, young fellow,
because I don't think it's going to last long in this sun.'

The moment Tris had departed with the children Laura
came downstairs and deposited herself on a kitchen chair.

'You look like Dracula's mother,' she remarked, as
Julia made coffee.

'Grandmother, even,' said Julia despondently.

Laura eyed her with sympathy. 'That bad, eh? I told
you it would hurt you more than all the Langs rolled
together.'

'Well, you were right there. I just couldn't bring myself
to do it when it came to the push.'

Laura looked unsurprised. She pushed back her mane
of corkscrew curls, and leaned her chin in her hands on

the table. 'I never really thought you would. So what now?'

'I don't know.'

'Do you intend doing something at a later date?'

'No. If I couldn't say anything last night I'm unlikely to say anything any other time either. I'm going to forget the whole thing and put it out of my mind. Forever.' Julia's face set in bleak lines. 'When it came to it I just couldn't keep to my "eye for an eye, tooth for a tooth" philosophy. Garrett and Claire Lang love each other so much it pervades their entire house, their whole life. I couldn't bring their house down like a pack of cards, perhaps affect their children—and Marcus.'

'Ah, Marcus. I had a feeling we'd find him in there somewhere.'

'He doesn't count. He was never part of my plan.'

'Don't tell me he hasn't influenced you in some way!'

Julia went out of the room and came back with the box containing the pearls. 'I suppose it was these that tipped the balance. Pearls for tears, they say. I suddenly woke up to all the tears and sorrow I'd cause if I spilled the beans. So I left the field to the enemy. The silly part of it all being that I can't see Garrett *as* the enemy, Marcus either, if it comes to that. And I certainly didn't want Claire wounded in the role of innocent civilian.'

'I'm glad,' said Laura.

'Yes, I know. You were always against it, weren't you?'

'Yes. And I didn't tell Tris everything, so if you want to fabricate some reason for the red eyelids, go ahead. I'll back you up.'

'Oh, Laura, you're a good friend. But don't have secrets from Tris. Tell him—I don't mind.' Julia jumped briskly to her feet. 'Right, that's enough of that. Let's get on with Christmas. If you make the mince pies, I'll do the stuffing for the turkey and wrestle with the vegetables.'

'Done!'

Marcus gave his employees the entire festive period off as a holiday, so it wasn't until the second day of the new year that Julia saw him again. And when she did she was rather sorry she had.

'What the hell's this?' he snarled, as he waved a letter at her.

'My resignation.'

'I managed to work out that much for myself! What I want to know is *why*?'

'I'm unable to go on working for you any longer,' said Julia, quaking inwardly.

'Let reception know we're not to be disturbed, then come into my office,' he snapped.

Julia did as he said and followed his tall figure across the room to their usual places. He slumped down into his chair and glared at her across the desk.

'I want reasons,' he said harshly.

Julia had none to give, and said so. 'My reasons are my own. Personal ones.'

'Are you pregnant?'

She glared at him in affront. 'Certainly not!'

'That's what's usually meant by "personal reasons".'

'Not in my case.'

'Do you want more money?'

'No.'

'Do you have a better job to go to? Has someone been poaching?'

'No.'

'Then what, woman? Tell me!' His eyes, ice-grey this morning, narrowed in a sudden gleam. 'Don't tell me it's because I kissed you.'

Julia said nothing. If that was what he wanted to think he was welcome to do so. And it was certainly a contributory factor, if not in the way he imagined.

'If I promise on the Bible never to do so again, would you stay?' he asked.

'I'm afraid not.'

His face set in bleak lines. 'You know, Julia, I could have sworn you and I were beginning to get on well, both here and socially. I thought you were one woman who was straight as a die. Yet here you are, like some Victorian maiden, ready to take off because I kissed you once. In rather special circumstances, I might add. It isn't as if I'm likely to chase you round your bloody desk!'

'I know that, Mr Lang.'

'For heaven's sake don't call me "Mr Lang"!' Marcus stared at her in frustrated rage. 'When do you want to go?'

'I'll wait until you find a replacement, then I'll stay until she's familiar with the job,' said Julia, avoiding his eyes.

'After which you bid me a fond farewell and I'll never see you again.'

Certainly not if I see you first, she thought miserably. 'I'm sorry for any inconvenience——'

'Inconvenience!' Marcus controlled himself with an effort, then leaned nearer. 'Julia, I wish you'd tell me what all this is about. I'm not thick, you know. It's obviously connected with whatever it was you tried to say the night of the dance.' He sat slumped in his chair, frowning at her. 'I've been thinking of it all over the holiday, almost rang you once or twice, to see if you were all right. But I was afraid you'd think I was sticking my nose in where it wasn't wanted.'

'Please,' said Julia desperately, 'can we just leave it? I'm sorry I'm forced to leave, but my decision is final. So can we just get on with the day's post now, please?'

Marcus looked at her drawn face in silence for a moment or two, then shrugged. 'Whatever you say,' he said heavily. 'Advertise for a replacement through the usual channels, but Julia, if it any time you change your mind don't let pride stop you saying so.'

'I shan't change my mind,' she said quietly.

'Then there's nothing more to be said.'

And true to his word, Marcus never referred to the subject again in the following days. Which was more than could be said for his brother. Garrett burst in to see her the same day, while his brother was out, demanding to know why she was leaving.

'Claire will be shattered! Why the hell do you want to leave?' he demanded.

'Personal reasons,' Julia repeated doggedly, and kept on repeating it to all and sundry who made it their business to question her on the subject.

'You knew how it would be,' said Laura later in the week. 'If his Miss Pennycook was with him for years, and only left at retiring age, it's not surprising everyone's amazed because you've thrown in the towel after only six months.'

'I just wish they'd accept it,' said Julia wearily, and put down the paper she was searching for job opportunities. 'I don't know why I'm looking in there, really.

I'll never find a job as interesting and well paid as this one.'

'So why leave it?'

'I must, Laura. I can't go on, day after day...' Julia's voice thickened, and she hurriedly snatched a tissue and blew her nose.

'All right, all right, love,' said the other girl hurriedly. 'You sort your own life out. I didn't mean to interfere.'

Julia smiled damply. 'Of course you don't interfere. Where would I be without you, Laura Murray?'

Life at Lang's was not easy over the next couple of weeks. Marcus went round with a face like carved granite, and everyone else seemed to Julia to be regarding her with reproach. Even Sam seemed more tiring than usual too, as if he sensed her troubled mind and was deliberately naughty. To her dismay he developed a worrying cough and she had trouble getting him off to sleep in the evenings. He took to waking several times in the night demanding water or merely a cuddle, with the result that Julia knew she looked like something the cat dragged in most mornings. Then Sam made a terrible fuss one day when she tried to hand him over to Laura, and by the time she arrived at Lang's she felt as if she'd been put through a mangle.

Marcus had taken care to avoid personal confrontation of any kind since Julia had told him she was leaving, but this morning he stared at her when she sat in her usual chair opposite him.

'Are you ill, Julia? You look terrible.'

'Just a bit tired,' she assured him.

'Burning the candle at both ends?'

What chance had she of that? thought Julia bitterly, but said nothing, merely looking pointedly at the pile of paperwork in front of him.

'I'm sorry, that was uncalled for.' He smiled at her suddenly, and to her horror she felt tears in her eyes at his unexpected sympathy. To her embarrassment they welled up and rolled down her cheeks, and with a murmured apology she fled in search of a handkerchief.

She had her face buried deep in the cupboard where she hung her coat, trying to pull herself together, when a crisp white handkerchief was thrust under her nose, and she was pulled into arms which held her close. It was too much. Her defences fell without a struggle and she yielded to an embrace whose comfort was so irresistible she was powerless against it. She was engulfed in her tears, drowned in them, and Marcus held her tightly until the storm of sobbing passed.

The door opened and a voice said, 'Mrs North, is the boss—oh, lord, I'm sorry!' And the door shut again, and Julia detached herself hurriedly from Marcus's arms and stared up at him in horror.

'Who was that?' she gasped.

'Dennis Hall from marketing,' he said, unperturbed.

Julia groaned. 'I'm so sorry—I don't know what on earth made me fall apart like that.'

'I think you do know. And I just wish you'd tell me what's tearing you in pieces like this, Julia.' He took her by the elbows and shook her slightly. 'Surely you can trust me?'

'I do trust you,' she said unsteadily, rubbing at her eyes. 'But there's nothing to tell. I'm just tired. Perhaps I'm coming down with a cold.'

Marcus thrust a hand distractedly through his hair. 'All right, if you won't tell me what's wrong heaven knows I can't force you.'

'And now it'll be all over the building that I was in your arms,' said Julia bitterly.

'Since you're leaving, I can't see that matters very much,' he retorted. 'Now, let's have some coffee, and when you feel up to it we'll get back to work.'

'Yes, of course.'

She had intended to go home for lunch, but because the delay in starting work had been her own fault she decided to ring Laura and say she'd work through and try to get home early. Laura told her Sam was asleep, anyway.

'At this time of day?' said Julia, surprised.

'Yes. He announced that he wanted bye-byes, so I put him in his cot, and Daisy and I are picnicking in your sitting-room in front of the television.'

Julia returned to her work station feeling a little worried, but put Sam from her mind as she concentrated on clearing the usual Monday work-load. She nipped out for a sandwich to eat at her desk, and when she returned Marcus was waiting for her in her office.

'There was a phone call for you, Julia,' he said quickly. 'A friend of yours, Laura Warren, said to tell you Sam was ill. Ring back now.'

Julia went white and dived for the telephone, her eyes apprehensive as Laura told her Sam had woken up crying and feverish.

'He's very hot, Julia. His temperature's sky-high, and he's crying for you. Do you think you can come home?'

'I'm on my way,' said Julia tersely.

'Trouble?' asked Marcus.

'Yes, Sam's ill. May I go now?'

'Of course.' He helped her on with her coat. 'I'll drive you.'

'Will you?' She stared at him abstractedly as she collected her things. 'How kind of you.'

The gleaming red Ferrari took them to Chester Road in a fraction of the time Julia would have taken to rush home, but even so she was in a fever of impatience to be out of the car almost before it had stopped, in no mood for conversation apart from the one question Marcus obviously couldn't prevent himself asking.

'Julia, who's Sam?'

She looked at him blankly. 'He's—he's a relative. Thank you for bringing me home. I'll make up the time tomorrow.'

Marcus brushed that aside, his eyes speculative as she tore away from him up the path and disappeared into the house.

Laura was walking up and down the sitting-room, trying to soothe a very hot, unhappy little boy. Sam stretched out his arms to Julia in entreaty as she burst into the room.

'Mummy, Mummy!'

Julia took him from Laura, cuddling him close and making little soothing sounds as the burning little body burrowed against her.

'He woke up like this,' said Laura anxiously. 'I sent Daisy upstairs on her own in case——'

'Of course—he's probably infectious! Very sensible.'

'I've rung for a doctor too.'

'Laura, you're an angel. Hush, darling, hush!' Julia rocked the little boy in her arms while Laura went off to make some tea, and after a while Sam quietened down enough for Julia to sit down on the sofa with him cradled in her arms. She managed a gulp or two of the tea Laura brought her, as the child dozed uneasily against her shoulder. 'I'll be fine now. You go off and see to Daisy.'

'I will, if you're sure you can manage.' Laura leaned over Sam uneasily. 'He's very flushed—I wonder what it is?'

'I think he's been simmering up for something all over the weekend. I haven't had a night's sleep for a while now, and he's been fiendishly crotchety. Anyway, Laura, off you go—and thanks. You'll get your reward one day.' Julia smiled at her friend gratefully.

It seemed hours before the doctor arrived, by which time Sam was crying pitifully again. Dr Phillips was someone Julia had known all her life, and he smiled at her in brisk reassurance as he told her to remove Sam's jersey and vest. To Julia's consternation the child's back and chest were covered in a fine red rash.

'Ah! Measles,' said the doctor.

'I never thought to look,' said Julia in remorse.

'Have to report it, I'm afraid. And you'll have a bit of a time with him for the next few days. He's likely to feel very poorly.' The doctor looked at her closely. 'You don't look all that good yourself, Julia.'

She explained about the disturbed nights.

'I'm afraid you'll have a few more before he's better. But he's a sturdy little chap, he'll soon be on the mend. If he doesn't settle get in touch, but I'll be back tomorrow to check on him in any case.'

Dr Phillips picked Sam up to allow Julia to get to her feet, and the little boy was promptly sick all down his sheepskin jacket.

'Don't worry, don't worry, Julia, I'm used to worse than that. It's not the first time the old coat has suffered, and probably won't be the last.'

Julia felt exhausted by the time the necessary mopping up was over and Sam was in clean pyjamas and wrapped in a blanket on the sofa. He seemed a little better after being sick, and lay listlessly watching her as she tidied up.

'Thirsty, Mummy,' he said drowsily, and Julia gave him a drink of soda water, shaking her head at Laura, who popped her head round the door.

'Don't come in, love, it's measles. And keep poor Daisy away. You won't want her coming down with it as well.'

'I should think she's likely to get it anyway, don't you?' Laura shrugged philosophically. 'Anyway, I'm just taking her to the shops, so is there anything you need?'

'Lots of things for Sam to drink, and some salad and ham for me, as I'm unlikely to have much time to spare for cooking for a while, the doctor informed me.'

The doctor was right. Sam, who had never been ill in his young life, apart from a spot of bother with teething, was not a good patient. Later that afternoon Julia rang Marcus and told him she needed time off to look after her invalid.

'Sam,' said Marcus.

'Yes.'

'I see—of course, take as much time as you want. I'll get someone from the typing pool to fill in.'

Julia thanked him, but her mind wasn't really on what he was saying. She had no thoughts to spare for anyone other than Sam, since his cough grew worse and made him throw up so often that she felt nervous about leaving him alone even for a second.

For the next few days she slept and ate very little, the thought of food extremely unappealing in the circumstances. The doctor called regularly and reassured her that the illness was running its usual course, and that Sam was doing as well as could be expected.

Marcus rang each day to enquire after the invalid, but with great restraint never asked again who Sam actually was, although it was obvious to Julia, even down a telephone line, that he badly wanted to find out.

Towards the end of the week Sam improved a little, and one evening went to sleep fairly early, with no objections about being left in his cot while Julia went to make herself some supper to eat on a tray in front of the television in the sitting-room. Afterwards, she decided, if Sam went on sleeping, she would wash her hair and do some ironing. But for the moment, while the lull lasted, she wanted nothing more than a poached egg on toast in front of some light entertainment.

She curled up on the sofa after she had eaten her egg, and pushed the tray to one side while she drank her coffee, half of her concentrated on the screen, the other half of her alert for any sound from Sam at the back of the house. A quiet knock on her door preceded Tristan's red head, which appeared round it enquiringly to ask after the invalid, and if there was anything he could do.

'Nothing, thanks,' Julia smiled gratefully.

'Laura feels guilty about not lending a hand.'

'Tell her to keep herself and Daisy well away. I think Sam's over the worst.' She frowned as the doorbell rang.

'Don't worry, I expect it's for me,' said Tristan. 'I'm doing a bit of coaching for a few weeks. That's probably one of my budding Picassos.'

Julia returned to her programme once she was sure the bell hadn't disturbed Sam, and looked up startled as Tristan ushered the tall figure of Marcus Lang into the room. Tris waved his hands in apology behind Marcus's back at the look of dismay on Julia's face.

'Visitor for you, love. See you later.' And Tris made himself scarce at top speed.

CHAPTER SEVEN

JULIA stared at her visitor in horror. Marcus looked enormous in her sitting-room in his belted tweed overcoat. Under it he wore one of his custom-made suits with a white shirt and sober silk tie. The slush of the street outside seemed to have made no impression on the gloss of his shoes, and he had taken time for his second shave of the day before coming to see her on his way home from Lang's. In the split second before she greeted him Julia became horribly aware of her lank hair and the circles under her eyes, of the streaks of congealed egg on the plate on the tray, the untidy room.

'Hello, Marcus,' she said, depressed rather than surprised. She'd known all along that a visit from him was on the cards, inevitable even. But not yet, and certainly not like this.

'Julia! What the hell have you been doing to yourself?' He strode across the room and jerked her to her feet, staring down into her face. 'Have you slept at all since I saw you last?'

She pulled away and collected her coffee-mug and the tray. 'Not much. Please sit down. I'm sorry I'm in such a mess. Can I get you a drink——' She stopped, frowning, not at all sure she had anything suitable to offer.

Marcus took the tray from her and dumped it on a table. 'I don't want a drink. I came to see how you were.'

'I'm fine.'

'You look it!'

She pushed a hand at her hair, colouring faintly. 'I haven't had much time for myself lately.' She looked down at herself, wishing she could sink through the floor. Her sweater had some of Sam's orange juice decorating the front, and her old cord jeans were rubbed at the knees. Her pink fluffy slippers added a final embarrassing footnote. She suppressed a shudder. Marcus must be wondering what had happened to his pin-neat Mrs North, who never had a hair out of place or a wrinkle in her skirt if she could help it.

'You've obviously had a rough time of it. Come and sit down again.' He led her to the sofa and sat down beside her. 'And how is this—this relative of yours, Julia? Sam, wasn't it? Is he any better?'

'Yes,' she said, praying fervently Sam wouldn't wake. 'Much better.'

'What was the trouble exactly?'

She thought rapidly. 'Oh, a—a sort of skin complaint.'

'A skin complaint.' Marcus's eyes, green tonight as bottle-glass, held hers against her will. 'Would you mind if I took my coat off, Julia?'

'No, of course not.' Oh, please don't let him stay long!

'What kind of skin complaint is it that flares up so suddenly you have to tear off from work at a moment's notice and then keeps you up at night looking after this Sam of yours?' Marcus leaned back in a corner of the sofa, watching her quizzically.

'I'm sorry I had to leave you in the lurch,' she said evasively. 'I'll come back as soon as he's well enough to be left.'

'Thank you. I've missed you. Not, unfortunately, that there's much point in my having you back if you're determined to leave me again as soon as possible,' he said wryly. 'And while we're on the subject, Julia, you might as well know now that I don't intend leaving here until I learn exactly what's driving you away from me.'

Julia sighed. 'Please, Marcus, there's no point in it now.'

'Now? What do you mean?' he said sharply.

'All you need to know is that I don't feel I can work for you any more and that's final.'

'Was that Sam who let me in?' he asked with sudden harshness.

Julia stared at him. 'No, of course not. I'm sorry, I should have introduced you. Tristan Murray lives upstairs.'

'He shares the house with you?'

The glitter in Marcus's eyes was so cold Julia felt a thrill of pleasure. He was jealous! She smiled faintly.

'Yes. So do his wife Laura and his daughter Daisy.'

Marcus scowled. 'Why didn't you say so straight away? Or do you enjoy watching me squirm?'

'Since I had no idea you were squirming, how could I?'

There was a simmering silence. Then Marcus said softly, 'But I still haven't learned the identity of the mysterious Sam.'

And right on cue a wail sounded from the back of the house. Julia jumped to her feet, giving Marcus a desperate look.

'Mummee——!' wailed Sam more loudly, and she fled, afraid the child would be sick before she reached him. She ran along the hall and into the small room next to hers, where Sam was standing in his cot, arms outstretched to her. 'Thirsty,' he said, and coughed a little, then coughed again deliberately, just in case Julia hadn't noticed. 'Juice,' he demanded.

'Juice, *please*,' said Julia automatically, 'but only if you go straight back to sleep again.' She poured the juice from a thermos jug and offered it to the little boy, waiting deliberately until he sat down.

Obediently Sam subsided, accepted the beaker and drank thirstily, then demanded a visit to the bathroom, which was such a recent accomplishment that Julia dared not ignore his request. It was some time before he was back in bed and settled down under his quilt.

'Owl and Pussy-Cat,' he ordered.

'You really are better, aren't you?' Julia said drily. 'If I sing will you go off to sleep like a good boy?'

He nodded triumphantly, and wriggled down under the covers as she sat on the rocking chair beside the cot to complete the required ritual. When it was over she went back into the sitting-room to Marcus, who sprang to his feet as she appeared, his eyes questioning in his set face.

Julia's shoulders drooped wearily. 'If you'll sit down and read the paper, Marcus, or watch television or something, I'll tidy myself up and then I'll come back and supply a few answers to the questions you naturally want to ask.'

'Thank you. I'd appreciate that,' he said with formality.

She bore the tray off to the kitchen, then hurried to her own room and changed her sweater and jeans for a pink wool shirt and black cord trousers. She brushed her hair furiously, added a touch of lipstick and put on flat black shoes instead of the embarrassing pink slippers, by which time Sam, to her profound relief, was asleep, deeply asleep, not the restless, twitching slumber of the past few days. Julia stood looking at him in silence, then straightened her shoulders and went back to rejoin Marcus.

'Would you like some coffee?' she asked, anxious to postpone the inevitable moment of truth.

He shook his head, looking grim. 'I have a feeling I'm likely to need something stronger than coffee once I've heard what you have to say. In the meantime, let's sit down and get on with it.' He took the chair opposite the sofa where she sat, and settled back with the air of a man intending to stay put until he knew all there was to know.

Julia found it very hard to begin. Marcus's face was unreadable, but by this time she knew him well enough to tell he was impatient to learn about Sam. So much so that as she hesitated he began for her.

'Is Sam your son, Julia?' he asked, as though the words were torn from him. 'Is that why you feel you must leave? Because you lied about having a child?'

'No, he's not *my* son,' she said, and to her surprise saw him relax, almost sag, as though a burden had been lifted from him. She smiled without humour. 'I've been a widow for almost six years. Sam is only a little over two years old.'

'I could tell that much from the way he sounded. Even so, it's not impossible to get pregnant even without a husband.'

'So you assumed he was illegitimate.' Julia gave him a very straight look. 'And you're right. But Sam's not my son, he's my nephew. And your brother Garrett is his father.'

It was almost bloodcurdling to witness the change in Marcus's manner. One moment his face held warmth and compassion, then the next it hardened to a coldness which made it appear carved from a block of marble.

'Oh, I see,' he said, his eyes full of the cynical boredom which had struck Julia so forcibly at their first encounter. 'So that was what it was all about—the big confrontation on the night of the office dance, I mean. You intended denouncing Garrett in front of his wife—accusing him of fathering this Sam of yours.' He took out a silver case and extracted a cigar. 'Do you mind if I smoke?'

'I'd rather you didn't. Sam has a cough, and the smoke might reach his room and start him off again.'

Marcus looked a trifle disconcerted for a moment as he replaced the case in his pocket. 'So why did you change your mind that night? An attack of conscience?'

'Conscience!' Julia's eyes flashed scornfully. '*My* conscience is clear. I changed my mind for the simple reason that after getting to know your brother better, and, more to the point as it happens, after becoming acquainted with Claire, whom I like very much, when it came to the push I just couldn't bring myself to wreck their lives after all. So I decided I'd just leave Lang's and bring up Sam the best way I can. I've managed in the past, and no doubt I'll manage in the future.'

'The child is nothing to do with Garrett, you know,' said Marcus quietly.

'Oh yes, he is. You haven't seen him. Sam's so like your nephew Charlie they could be brothers. Which they are,' added Julia defiantly, 'whatever you say.'

Marcus stared at her in hostile silence for so long she began to feel hunted, then he shrugged. 'All right. Tell me the story from the beginning. No frills, just facts, please. I don't promise to believe you, but I'll hear you out.'

Julia's face flamed with anger. 'I'm really not interested in whether you believe me or not, Marcus Lang. I've given up all idea of making Sam's presence known to your family, I no longer intend working for you, so once you go through that door you don't have to give Sam, or me, another thought, I promise.'

'As easy as that,' he said bitterly, then his eyes narrowed. 'Is that why you applied for the job, by the way? To worm your way into my confidence, make yourself so necessary to me——'

Julia shook her head. 'You yourself had nothing at all to do with it. It was Garrett I wanted to get at. I'd never met him, you understand, but my motivation for applying for a job at Lang's was purely to——' She stopped short, as Marcus sprang to his feet and stood over her menacingly.

'So I was totally irrelevant to your little plan, whatever it was! A mere accessory to your little game.' He flung away to the fireplace and stood staring down into the imitation gas coals flickering there, his back eloquent with disgust.

'I never aspired to a job as your personal assistant, Marcus,' said Julia evenly. 'Any job would have done, as long as I had the entrée into the firm. It seemed as if fate was on my side when I heard that Miss Pennycook was leaving. Even more so when you chose me for the job.'

He turned, smiling mirthlessly. 'Twenty or more applicants and I had to choose you, Julia North. This fate of yours must have been in a very skittish mood the day I first laid eyes on you.'

'I never intended to cause trouble for you——'

'Are you serious? Do you actually believe you could wreck Garrett and Claire's life without affecting *me*?' He glared at her in cold fury. 'What kind of woman *are* you, Julia?'

She glared back, then jerked her head towards the large photograph which hung on the wall. 'That's the kind of woman I used to be, if it's of any interest to you.'

Marcus swung round to examine the photograph, which showed a young, laughing girl in a white lace dress and wide-brimmed hat. Her hair rioted under the hat in a mass of curls and her hand lay on the arm of a young man in conventional morning suit, a top hat in the crook of his free arm, his face alight with tenderness as he smiled down at his bride.

'Richard and I on our wedding day,' Julia explained. 'Young and carefree, with no idea of what lay ahead of us. Just as well, as it happened. Not long afterwards Richard was killed in a train derailment. Sad little story, isn't it?' she added huskily.

'You've changed,' said Marcus. 'Your hair is straight now.'

'It was straight then. But I used to have it layered and permed into the mane you can see there. Richard liked it that way. I did too,' she said pensively.

Marcus turned to look at her. 'Then why did you change it?'

'To alter my image. To transform myself into the perfect secretary.' Julia smiled faintly. 'Oh, I know some men still hanker for a nubile young creature with long legs and more talent for making coffee than typing, but I knew it would be different at Lang's.'

Marcus looked at her levelly. 'Not much. Both your legs and your coffee are excellent, Julia.'

'But that isn't why you engaged me.'

'No.'

Their eyes held for a moment, then Marcus resumed his seat. 'Go on, Julia. Say what you have to say.'

She curled up in a corner of the sofa and steeled herself to begin the story she had always intended to tell one day. But to Garrett Lang, not Marcus. She tried to tell it dispassionately, as though it were fiction, and nothing to do with herself or Sam. Or Sam's mother.

She began by describing the parents who had been a happy, loving couple, their lives shadowed only by the fact that the child they longed for never materialised. Eventually they gave up and adopted a baby girl of only a few weeks old. By the time they took possession of Julia they were no longer young, but ecstatically happy with their 'chosen' child, and quite unprepared for the shock, four years later, when they found they were to have a child of their own. Elizabeth arrived at a time when most couples were expecting grandchildren, but her advent was no less joyfully anticipated and welcomed by the entire family.

'I loved having a baby sister,' said Julia, looking into the fire. 'She was so tiny and fragile I used to hang over her cot and marvel at her fingernails and the pulse throbbing in her soft little head. I adored her.'

The family was a very happy one with the addition of the blonde, bubbling Elizabeth, but the latter was still in school when the blow fell on the close-knit Hughes family.

'Not long after I met Richard—I was just finishing in training college by this time—my parents died within a few months of each other,' said Julia.

'So you were left with the responsibility of your sister,' said Marcus with sympathy.

'Yes. They'd made wills years before, of course, dividing everything between us, so we decided to sell the family house, which was larger than this, then with my half of the money, plus Richard's contribution, we bought this one. Richard and I got married and made a home for my sister with us, and put her legacy into investments for her.'

But then Richard had been killed, and Julia had to pick up the pieces of her life once again. Money was short, but Julia refused to dip into her sister's nest-egg, so Elizabeth took a secretarial course and afterwards managed to get herself a job at Lang's.

Marcus looked across at her sharply. 'She worked for us?'

Julia nodded. 'Yes—in a very junior capacity in the typing pool. She loved it. She adored being independent, and when I took in the Murrays as tenants she coaxed me to let her share a flat in town with some other girls. I hadn't the heart to say no, but of course from then on obviously I knew less about how she spent her time than before, though I made it a rule that she came round here every Sunday, so I could make sure she was all right, and see she ate a civilised meal once a week.'

Julia paused, her throat dry. 'Shall we have some coffee?' she suggested.

Marcus nodded. 'Thank you. Can I help?'

'No, thanks, I shan't be long.' She badly needed a moment or two to herself and lingered a moment in

Sam's room, watching his flushed, sleeping face, before she took a tray back to the sitting-room.

Marcus sprang up to take the tray from her, and set it down on a low table at the end of the sofa, then he sat down beside her as she began to pour. Suddenly she was deeply aware of his physical presence. She could smell the cologne he sometimes used, rather sharp and astringent, in keeping with his personality. She could feel the warmth of his body as his thigh casually brushed hers, and shifted uneasily, wishing he would move back to the chair again.

'I'm sorry I can't offer you a brandy,' she said, desperate to break the sudden pregnant silence.

'I don't need brandy,' he said softly, and touched a hand to her cheek. 'You're the one who looks in need of it, not me.'

Julia drew away, dismayed to find herself trembling at his touch. 'I'm suffering from a few sleepless nights, that's all.'

'So am I.'

The words were flung down like a challenge and her eyes flew to his face in surprise. As she met the heat in his eyes she clenched her teeth to control a sudden tremor of apprehension.

'Overwork?' she asked brightly.

'No.' Marcus took the coffee-cup from her and put it on the tray. 'I miss you, Julia.' He moved closer and slid an arm round her waist, locking his eyes with hers. 'Come back to me,' he said urgently. 'I don't need to hear this story of yours. I don't care if you came to work for me with some crazy idea of revenge. I just want you back. That's why I'm here.'

Julia stared up at him, bemused. He meant it—he really meant it. He didn't care about her plan to discredit Garrett.

'You must see that's impossible,' she said breathlessly. 'Now you know about Sam——'

'Julia, I don't care about Sam.' Suddenly Marcus pulled her into his arms and spoke with his lips almost touching hers. 'All I know is that I want you back. Only a short time without you has been enough to drive me mad.' And he kissed her in a way which stopped any further argument.

Julia was too tired to resist. But not too tired to respond, she found. His mouth, that firm, controlled mouth she knew so well, was very expert in caressing her own into trembling acquiescence. Then the acquiescence changed and she was kissing him back, conscious in every nerve of the dangerous feeling of a haven she'd been searching for and at long last found. At the thought she trembled, and Marcus held her even more tightly, bending to scoop her up on to his lap as easily as though she were Sam. Holding her cradled against him, he let his lips rove all over her face until they met her expectant mouth, and Julia made a little smothered sound. A great shiver ran through her as she felt his tongue seek out the secret places of her mouth. Marcus groaned and raised his head to look down into her flushed, heavy-eyed face, then began kissing her again, purposefully this time, his hands coaxing and caressing as they moved over the curves outlined by her thin wool sweater.

'Julia, I want you,' he gasped at last, rubbing his cheek against hers, 'do you want me? For Pete's sake tell me you do.'

Julia shivered against him. 'I do—you know very well I do. But, Marcus, I can't let you make love to me.'

'Why not?' he demanded, eyes glittering. 'We're adults, and not exactly strangers. And you know damn well that this thing between us has been growing stronger ever since the day I first saw you walk into my office. Why else do you think I chose you from all the others?'

Julia removed herself from his grasp with a sudden wrench, and resumed her seat in the sofa corner, glaring at him. 'I thought you chose me because I was likely to be an efficient replacement for your matchless Miss Pennycook!'

'There were at least half a dozen others who would have done just as well, and most of them were a lot more experienced than you, my darling Mrs North.'

The indulgence in his smile flicked Julia on the raw.

'I see,' she said tightly. 'Then I'm glad my resignation won't cause too much inconvenience. It seems unlikely you'll have difficulty in replacing me.'

Marcus took her hands in his, the smile fading. 'I don't want anyone else. I want you.'

'You don't employ women burdened with demanding children, remember!'

'But Sam's not yours.'

'In every way except the accident of conception and birth he is, believe me. I'm all the mother he's got.'

Marcus subsided against the sofa cushions, frowning. 'I heard him call you "Mummy".'

'He calls Laura "Mummy" too. Sam thinks it's a collective name for all women.' Julia pushed a hand through her hair. 'Anyway, I promised Libby I'd look after him——'

'Libby?' Marcus shot out a hand to imprison hers, his eyes suddenly piercing as they met hers. 'Who's Libby?'

Julia pulled her hand away, rubbing at the marks his fingers had made. 'My sister Elizabeth—Sam's mother. Why, what's the matter?' she said quickly, as Marcus's face lost colour.

'Her other name?' he asked harshly.

'Hughes.' Julia looked at him searchingly. 'Do you remember her? I wouldn't have thought so. She worked in the fish tank—the typing pool, I mean—but you were away in the States for most of the time she was there. It was Garrett she always talked about. She worked for him for two weeks while his secretary was on holiday, and never stopped talking about him. But she never mentioned you. It was "Mr Lang" all day long, goodness knows, but it was Garrett she meant. To her he was the only "Mr Lang" in the firm.'

Suddenly the door began to open, and Julia sprang up as Sam appeared in the opening, rubbing his eyes as he coughed.

'I *called*, Mummy,' he said indignantly, and yawned. 'You didn't come.'

Julia picked him up hurriedly, flushing as Marcus rose to his feet, his eyes incredulous on the little boy's face. 'Back to bed, Sam. You'll catch cold.'

'Who's that?' asked the child suspiciously, pointing at Marcus.

'I'm a friend of your mummy,' said Marcus softly, plainly unable to take his eyes off Sam, who glared back jealously, comically hostile towards the man taking up Julia's attention.

'Come on,' said Julia firmly. 'Bed for you, young man, and no nonsense.'

Sam coughed experimentally as she bore him off, but Julia was in no mood to be conned, and tucked him up with an expression on her face Sam obviously recognised as immovable. He settled down obediently, yawning again as she leaned down to kiss him goodnight.

'Don't like the man,' he muttered sleepily.

'He's just leaving,' Julia assured him, and went quietly from the room.

Marcus was standing where she'd left him in the middle of the room, looking like a man in shock.

'Now do you believe me?' she demanded. 'He's the image of Charlie, isn't he? And Claire assures me that's exactly how Garrett looked at the same age.'

'He did,' agreed Marcus. 'Nevertheless, your Sam isn't Garrett's child.'

Julia closed her eyes in frustration, then opened them at him angrily. 'What does it take to convince you, Marcus Lang? Sit down—please—and I'll try to round off my little tale.'

She told him how Libby had come home starry-eyed the first day she had caught a glimpse of Garrett Lang, and stayed that way all the time she worked for Lang Holdings. Julia grew sick and tired of hearing how wonderful Mr Lang was, how much everyone liked him, how kind he was to Libby when she ran errands for him, or took up his post. In Libby's eyes he could do no wrong, until the night of the Lang Christmas party, which was held that year in a hotel in the Cotswolds. Libby had been exuberant with excitement about it, and took Julia off with her weeks beforehand to help choose a dress

Libby felt would make her look sophisticated and really grown up.

'She dressed here that night, and went off looking radiant in her new black dress, every blonde hair gleaming, her eyes shining like candles on the Christmas tree,' said Julia, staring down at her hands. 'But she came back early in a taxi, said she'd felt tired, and spent the next day, Christmas Eve, in bed. It worried me quite a lot at the time, because it was so unlike her. Normally Libby had enough energy for two.' She looked up sharply as Marcus made a sudden involuntary movement beside her.

'Go on,' he said harshly.

'There's not much more to tell. To my surprise Libby said she'd had a quarrel with one of the other girls and didn't want to work at Lang's any more. She gave in her notice after Christmas and asked would it be all right if she came back home for a while, because she felt like a rest before looking for another job. I was back at the school by then, and liked having her there when I came home, although I could never get her to tell me why she left her beloved job at Lang's. After a couple of months, of course, it became obvious. She was pregnant.' Julia's eyes hardened as she described the day her sister had confided her news with such desperation in her big blue eyes, confessing how afraid she was, but resolutely refusing to give Julia the name of the father. All she would say was that the man was already married, and became so hysterical if her sister pressed the point that Julia gave up questioning her on the subject.

'It was a nerve-racking time. Our doctor was very worried about her because she developed a toxic condition, she was constantly nauseated, and in the end she went into labour over a month early. The labour was hard, and Libby was utterly exhausted afterwards. But not too exhausted to make me promise I'd never tell the father of the baby if she told me his name. Almost as though she—she knew.' Julia swallowed hard. 'In the end she admitted that "Mr Lang" was responsible. The man she'd been so crazy about.' Julia took a deep, unsteady breath. 'That night she suffered a fatal brain haemorrhage. There was nothing anyone could have done to save her.'

Marcus got to his feet with an effort that made Julia stare. He seemed to have aged ten years in the space of as many minutes. He rose to his full height and looked down at her with dull, lightless eyes.

'You said Sam is just over two years old.'

'Yes. He'll be three in September.'

'Then he can't possibly be Garrett's child, Julia. Claire had such a hard time with Charlie's birth that Garrett had a vasectomy about four years ago.' Marcus took in a deep, unsteady breath. 'Not that I'm disputing Sam's Lang blood—the eyes and the likeness are unmistakable. But I'm afraid Charlie and Garrett aren't the only ones Sam resembles, Julia; I have old photographs of myself which prove he's also the image of me at the same age.'

'You!' Julia stared at him in horror.

Marcus nodded, looking haggard. 'Whatever vengeance you had planned was misdirected, Julia. Garrett's not the guilty party. I am.'

CHAPTER EIGHT

JULIA rose very slowly to her feet, her eyes holding his incredulously. 'What are you talking about? You didn't even know Libby.'

'No, I didn't.'

'Then how can you be the father of her child?'

Marcus looked ashen as he eased a finger inside his collar. 'I suppose I'd better start at the beginning. I flew back from the States the day before the party to find my wife wanted a divorce.'

Julia turned away sharply, hugging her arms across her chest. How could she have forgotten Marcus once had a wife!

'The news was a bitter blow,' Marcus went on heavily. 'I was angry. Nicola told me there was another man, one who was likely to pay more attention to her than I ever had. I was furious. I flatly refused to divorce her. The row went on for hours. Then next day we were both expected to pin smiles on our faces and attend the usual Christmas party for the employees at Lang's.' He put a hand on Julia's shoulder, but she shrugged it off. 'At least turn round and face me, please. I don't like talking to the back of your head.'

Since it was the last time Julia ever intended him to talk to her at all she turned round as Marcus asked.

'Go on,' she said quietly.

'In my misery I drank more than usual that night, and at some stage in the proceedings was obliged to ask the hotel manager if he had an unoccupied room I could rest in for a while to get over what I described as jet-lag. I didn't mention the rage and humiliation and jealousy mixed in with it from Nicola's rejection.' Marcus's voice grated with self-derision. 'I lay on the bed in the dark in that room, with a bottle of Bollinger for company, so submerged in self-pity I never even no-ticed when the door opened and someone came in. It was only when a feminine body slid close in the dark, and two arms twined around me, that I realised I had feminine company. The perfume I could smell was one my wife used, and I honestly believed it was Nicola, come to tell me it had all been a mistake, that she loved me and still wanted me. I suppose I wanted to believe it. In the darkness, in the haze of weariness and alcohol, all I knew was that I had a soft, urgent body in my arms, a mouth on mine that was willing, and hands that—that enticed.'

Julia stared at him in sick affront. *'Libby?'*

'Yes. Not that I knew that until afterwards. At first I was oblivious of anything other than the balm I was receiving to my male ego.' Marcus paused, breathing in deeply as he rubbed a hand over his mouth. 'Then at a certain stage in the proceedings my mistake became all too evident, because I discovered that the girl in my arms was—inexperienced. But by then, of course, the damage was done.'

Julia gave an anguished little moan.

He held up his hands, shrugging. 'I'm telling it like it was, Julia. I'm not decrying your sister, or excusing myself. It all happened like a dream up to a point. Then my ego took another knock when I came to my senses enough to realise that the name she was saying over and over again was "Garrett".' He shuddered. 'I'll never forget the look of horror on the child's face when I switched on the light and she saw who I was. She began to cry like a lost soul. I tried to reassure her, to comfort her, whereupon my lady wife finally *did* put in an appearance and found me with a dishevelled, hysterical girl in my arms.'

Julia felt sick. 'What happened then?' she whispered.

Marcus breathed in heavily. 'Nicola made very little fuss, to be fair. I think she was grateful to the—to your sister. I had no hope of contesting the divorce after the scene my wife interrupted. In fact she was the one who mopped up the horrified child, ordered a taxi, and saw to it that your sister's friends believed she'd been taken ill.'

'While you just stood by.'

Marcus nodded bleakly. 'I had no choice. The revulsion in that child's face when she realised I was the wrong man has haunted my dreams ever since, believe me. She implored me not to tell Garrett, said he had no idea how she felt, hardly knew she existed.'

Julia turned cold, angry eyes on his face. 'Did you never wonder what happened to Libby afterwards?'

'Of course I did! I tried to get in contact with her at the address Personnel gave me, but got no reply. I asked Miss Pennycook to make enquiries among her friends in the typing pool, but all she learned was that Libby Hughes had left her flat, and none of her flatmates would admit they knew where she'd gone.'

'She must have sworn them all to silence,' said Julia bleakly.

'In the end I gave up.' Marcus looked grim. 'After all, Julia, I was certain that any girl in that particular

set of circumstances would have been only too quick to
contact me for financial compensation if she became
pregnant. I'm not proud of myself, believe me, but I
assure you I did my best to trace her. When I couldn't
I assumed there had been no consequences to the episode, and that the poor child wanted the whole thing
kept quiet. And then I was taken up with the trauma of
my divorce, and a couple of crises in the course of
running Lang's, and I'm ashamed to say that eventually
I imagined the whole thing was over and done with.'

Julia sat down abruptly. 'Which, as far as you're concerned, of course, it was.'

Marcus dropped on one knee in front of her and took
her hands, looking up urgently into her hostile eyes. 'But
now I know what's happened I assume full responsibility, Julia. I want to make up for all the hardship you've
suffered——'

'How do you propose to make up to Libby?' she said
cruelly, and watched as the colour drained from his face.
He dropped her hands and got wearily to his feet.

'I can't, of course. All I can do is provide for her
son—and mine,' he added, his eyes kindling suddenly.
'Sam is *my* son too, remember. I have a right——'

'*Right!*' said Julia with scorn. 'A couple of blind, un-
thinking moments in the dark give you a right to Sam!
No way, Marcus Lang. Libby left Sam in my care, and
that's where he'll stay.'

Marcus stood over her menacingly. 'So what happened to the woman who plotted her way into Lang
Holdings to blackmail my brother about the very same
child?'

Julia flushed. 'I came to my senses, that's all. I was
out of my mind with grief and resentment after Libby

died. Grief over her death, and resentment, I'm ashamed to say, because I was the one left holding the baby. The urge for revenge was so strong I asked Laura to take care of the baby on a paying basis so I could keep my teaching job and go to secretarial classes in the evenings when Sam was in bed. I set out very deliberately to transform myself into the perfect clerical employee for Lang Holdings when the moment arrived. I let my curls grow out and had my hair cut; it wasn't difficult to look more mature. Broken nights with a crying baby, and lots of walks with a pram, soon put paid to any puppy fat left from Julia North's girlhood, believe me. The life of a single parent is no picnic, Marcus Lang. Particularly when motherhood, like greatness, is thrust upon one.'

'And all along your motivation in getting a job with Lang's was to confront Garrett one day with the truth about Sam,' said Marcus quietly.

Julia nodded. 'The thought of him, happy with his wife and children while poor Libby was dead, was like a goad urging me on.'

'Why didn't you simply appear at his house with the baby in your arms in true melodrama tradition and present him with the proof of his perfidy?'

Her eyes flashed at the note of dryness in Marcus's voice. 'Oh, I wanted more than that. You have no idea just how much revenge I had in mind. I had wild ideas about industrial espionage, tampering with records to discredit Garrett's name professionally, all sorts of things before the final dénouement.'

'How did you intend to manage all that?' asked Marcus, frowning.

Julia bit her lip and turned her head away from his searching eyes. 'I have no idea. Seems silly now, doesn't it? Looking back, I realise how unbalanced I was over the whole thing.' She gave a mirthless little laugh. 'Laura Murray, who knows me pretty well by now, never thought for a moment I'd carry out my stupid plan. And she was right. Almost the first time I met Garrett I knew I'd never be able to do it. In fact the moment I began working for you I realised I had no hope of sabotaging anything at the firm.'

'You could have, quite easily. Some of the things you deal with are highly confidential.'

Julia looked at him ruefully. 'I knew from the start you were not the man to tangle with, Marcus. But then, you see, I never anticipated working for the boss man himself.'

'Then what the hell did you imagine you'd achieve as a more ordinary cog in the machinery?'

'Since it's all academic now, I don't see much point in discussing it any further,' said Julia, suddenly feeling weary. 'Please leave now, Marcus. I'm very tired.'

'I can see that.' Marcus leaned down and took her by the hands, pulling her to her feet, close to him, so that their joined hands formed the only physical barrier between them. 'I meant what I said, Julia. I miss you. Come back to me.'

'That's out of the question! Good lord, now you know about Sam how could we possibly achieve a feasible working relationship?' Julia wrenched her hands away, but Marcus caught her by the shoulders and kissed her, taking her by surprise.

'I don't want a working relationship,' he muttered against her mouth. 'I just want you.' And his arms closed round her, his lips parting hers forcefully, demanding a response she fought to deny him. She failed utterly, her mouth opening to his as he held her tightly with one arm, his mouth still against hers as he shrugged off his jacket before drawing her down with him to the sofa. Suddenly Julia forgot Sam, forgot Libby, conscious only of the sudden clamouring of her body which burned for the caresses of the man holding her close.

At the first touch of his fingers on her throat she shivered, and arched her body closer. Marcus undid her shirt and laid his lips to the hollow between her breasts, and her shivering intensified as he reached behind her to release the catch that allowed his lips access to the breasts which hardened in response to his touch, pushing themselves shamelessly into the palms of his hands as he cupped them reverently before taking one of the erect tips into his mouth.

Julia moaned and moved her head back and forth against the sofa cushions, her hips thrusting upwards involuntarily as his body moved over hers. Marcus brought his mouth down hard on hers, his fingers shaking as they tried to unfasten the buckle of her wide leather belt. And Julia's mind switched on again abruptly. She pushed violently at him, sitting up and swinging her feet to the ground in one convulsive movement.

'Julia—for goodness' sake,' he said, his voice rasping and unsteady. 'Do you want to drive me insane?'

'No,' she said dully, looking at the carpet between her feet. 'I just want you to go.'

Marcus sprang to his feet, tucking his shirt in and rescuing his tie. His face was angry and set as he resumed his jacket and shrugged into his overcoat, tying the belt with a violent jerk. 'So you're a teaser, Julia.'

'No, I'm not.' She got to her feet wearily, pushing at her untidy hair as she met his eyes. 'But I don't—I don't indulge in that sort of thing. I freely admit I lost my head for a moment or two, and for that I apologise. I should have made it clear from the start that I don't have lovers.'

Marcus rolled up his silk tie and stuffed it into a pocket. 'Do you think I don't know that? I just want you to have one lover, Julia. In the singular. Myself. And you wanted me then just as much as I wanted you.'

Julia nodded. 'My body was all for it, I grant you. Fortunately my mind woke up again before I reached the point of no return.'

Marcus took her by the elbows, his eyes dark now as he stared down at her. '*Why*, Julia? Why won't you let me make love to you?'

'I would have thought it obvious! For one thing, I can do without another little addition to my life. And for another, you're the man who was, however accidentally, responsible for my sister's death. As lovers, Marcus,' she added scathingly, 'I don't feel we have too much going for us, do you?'

'Who was the visitor last night?' asked Laura next morning. 'And don't tell me to go away, because I'm sure Sam's no longer infectious, and anyway I've left Daisy upstairs with Tris, and I've had measles. So tell me.'

'Marcus Lang,' whispered Julia, shutting the bedroom door. 'Sam's gone back to bed this morning. Catching up on his lost sleep.'

'You look as if you could do with a nap yourself.'
Laura went into the kitchen and filled the kettle. 'Sit
down, Julia—I'll do this. You look terrible!'

'I feel it.' Julia flopped down at the table and leaned
her chin in her hands. 'Sam woke and Marcus saw him.'

Laura waited expectantly. 'And?' she prompted.

Julia gave her a carefully edited version of the events
of the night before, leaving out any mention of lovemaking. Although thoughts of Marcus's lips and hands
had kept her awake half the night, this morning she
couldn't even bear to think of them. Her mind was completely monopolised by the incredible fact that Sam owed
his existence not to Garrett Lang, but to Marcus.

'It takes some getting used to, Laura,' she said
pensively.

Laura set down two mugs of coffee, her eyes like
saucers. 'Thank heaven you never actually got round to
denouncing Garrett Lang, Julia! Not that I ever thought
for a moment you actually would,' she added.

'Why not?'

'Because by this time, Julia North, I know perfectly
well you just don't have it in you to go round wrecking
people's lives.'

'Unlike Marcus Lang,' said Julia tartly, and drank
some coffee.

'Be fair, Julia. You said he tried to contact Libby
afterwards.'

'I know, I know.'

'And what does he intend to do now?'

'He said something about taking care of Sam and me,'
muttered Julia, refusing to meet the other girl's eyes.

'And what did you say to that?'

In her present state of exhaustion Julia wasn't at all clear what she'd said, only that in the end she'd told Marcus to go away, to stay out of her life—and Sam's.

'You're not serious!' said Laura in disgust. 'Surely if the man offered——'

'I don't want to talk about it!' said Julia, with such a look of torment on her face that Laura jumped up and put an arm round her shoulders.

'Now listen, Julia, I want you to go and soak in a bath for ages, then go to bed. Tris is taking Daisy over to his mother's for the day, so I shall stay down here and make a start on the tapestry I got for Christmas, and you're going upstairs into my bed and you're going to stay there until you look like a human being again.'

'But, Laura——'

'But nothing. I'll just pop up to see Tris is putting her new dress on Daisy, then I'll be back.' And with a toss of her corkscrew curls Laura was gone before Julia could summon up the strength to argue.

It was wonderful to lie as long as she liked in steaming, scented water, to feel her hair squeaky clean again, and even more wonderful to climb into the Murrays' wide bed, freshly made up for the occasion with the crisp white sheets Laura kept for visitors. Julia slid between them with a great sigh, secure in the knowledge that Sam was safe in Laura's slender, clever hands. Not even the revelations of the night before had any power to keep Julia from the sleep that claimed her almost at once, giving her a temporary respite from the new set of problems fate had landed in her lap.

When she woke it was mid-afternoon. She jumped out of bed in dismay and threw on her dressing gown as she ran like the wind down the stairs to her own part of the house. The scene in the sitting-room was peaceful. Sam was sitting on a rug in the middle of the room, absorbed in moving the animals about on the largest toy farm Julia had ever seen. He beamed up at Julia, tightening his grasp possessively on the sheep he was arranging in one of the fields surrounding his farm.

'You look a lot better,' said Laura approvingly.

Julia hardly heard her. 'Where did that come from?' she demanded, pointing at the farm.

'Farm,' said Sam, coughing a little. '*My* farm,' he added, just in case Julia was under any misapprehension.

'It arrived this morning by messenger,' said Laura, 'and since it was addressed to Sam I thought I'd unpack it. Hope you don't mind.' She wore a slightly guilty look as she grinned up at Julia. 'It's certainly kept him quiet!'

'I don't have to ask who sent it,' said Julia, her eyes flashing. 'Did it say "From Daddy with love"?'

'No.' Laura held up a familiar card printed with the name 'Marcus Lang' and nothing else.

'You'd better go and look in the kitchen,' said Laura. 'I didn't quite know what to do with the offering you got.'

Julia went to the kitchen—and stopped dead in the doorway. Every available receptacle she possessed was full of flowers. Roses, carnations, early daffodils and tall blue spears of iris occupied plastic buckets, the kitchen sink, china bowls. Propped up against one of the bowls was another of Marcus's cards, in an envelope this time. Above his name Marcus had written 'Come back to me'. She stared at his familiar handwriting, hugging her arms round her chest. Last night she'd told him to go in no uncertain terms. She'd hardly slept afterwards, shedding bitter tears because she didn't want him to go, tears because he was the one responsible for Sam's birth and Libby's death, and it was impossible even to consider a relationship with him. Even though she was in love with him. Julia winced. There, she'd admitted it. If it weren't for Sam and Libby, last night would have been a different story. Right there in the sitting-room, where Sam was playing so happily now, Julia knew she would have let Marcus make love to her, for the simple reason that she loved him and wanted him to make love to her so badly it had torn her apart to send him away.

'Quite a show, isn't it?' said Laura behind her, and Julia blinked, pulling herself together.

'A bit over the top,' she agreed. 'And a bit late to send them all back by this time.'

'If you did you'd have to send the farm back too, wouldn't you say?' Laura made a face. 'If you do, please let me get upstairs before you break the news to Sam!'

Julia quickly began arranging flowers, searching in cupboards for vases and jugs brought from her mother's house. 'You shouldn't have unwrapped it, Laura.'

'I'm sorry. I'm an interfering busybody, I know, but I thought it might do some good in the long run.' Laura began clearing leaves and twigs into the waste-bin. 'Marcus Lang could do a lot for Sam, you know.'

'I do know. But I can't forget Libby.' Julia thrust an armful of flowers at Laura. 'Here, take these—I don't have room for them all.' Her eyes softened. 'And thanks, Laura—for everything. There should be more busybodies like you!'

Sam improved quickly over the next few days, while Julia kept waiting for Marcus to make another move. She deliberately made no acknowledgement of his gifts, reluctant to initiate any contact with him, and as the days went by she began to think that Marcus intended to take her at her word and leave her—and Sam—alone. She began searching the newspapers in earnest for suitable jobs, but without success, and began to feel the first stirrings of genuine fear for the future. Her only ray of light was the fact that Sam improved steadily.

'He's as fit as a fiddle,' said Dr Phillips eventually. 'I shan't need to come again.'

Julia looked at him searchingly. 'Doctor, Sam's really all right, is he? I mean, there's no possibility of anything happening to him like—like Libby?'

Dr Phillips shook his head decisively. 'None at all. Elizabeth's death was tragic—one of nature's cruel accidents, nothing at all to do with Sam.' He patted her cheek kindly. 'Try not to fret about it, Julia. You've got enough on your plate just looking after young Sam.'

Julia was very thoughtful after Dr Phillips had gone. Sam looked up hopefully from his farm as she went back into the room.

'Go out, Mummy?'

'Not yet. In a day or two, the doctor said. Shall I read to you?'

Sam shook his curly brown head. 'Play with my farm. On my alone,' he added, as Julia prepared to join him. She sat down on the sofa, feeling oddly rebuffed, at a loss for something to do in the first time for months. She picked up a book, but the words made no sense, so she switched on the television. She tried to concentrate on an interview with the author of a best-seller she wanted to read, but the lady was so erudite Julia found the conversation totally beyond her present state of abstraction.

My mind must be atrophying from lack of use, she thought bitterly, and stared down at Sam, who was completely absorbed in running a tiny tractor over the fields of his new agricultural domain. The doorbell startled her out of her reverie. She was even more startled when she learned the identity of her visitor. Claire Lang stood on the doorstep, smiling a little warily, as though uncertain of her welcome.

'Hello, Julia. Is this a bad moment? May I come in?'

'Why, Claire, how very nice to see you!' Julia's brain worked at top speed as she ushered Claire inside and opened the door to the sitting-room. Was she an emissary from Marcus? Did she know about Sam? Most important of all, from Julia's point of view, did she know just what Julia's intentions had been regarding Garrett?

Claire answered one of the questions by smiling delightedly down at Sam when he scrambled to his feet at the sight of the pretty lady.

'Hello, Sam,' she said airily. 'Are your measles all gone?'

He nodded. 'I was *awful* sick,' he informed her proudly.

'How nasty,' said Claire sympathetically. 'My little boys have had measles too.'

'Were they sick?' asked Sam with interest.

'Perhaps not as sick as you,' said Claire with tact. 'But more than enough for me,' she added ruefully to Julia. 'I don't know about you, but I feel I've aged at least ten years in the past couple of weeks.'

'I'm sorry about the boys,' said Julia awkwardly. 'Let me make you some tea. My good fairy Laura—Laura Murray who shares the house—did some shopping today, so we have chocolate biscuits and some sticky buns to offer.'

'Heavenly!' Claire looked down at Sam as he returned to his sheep and cows. 'Will it be all right if I come and help?'

It was evident she wanted to talk.

'He'll soon let us know if he's bored,' said Julia. 'Come on through to the kitchen.'

Claire began without beating about the bush, as Julia filled the kettle. 'To save any misunderstandings, Marcus told us everything, Julia.'

Julia's fingers were unsteady as she plugged the lead into the socket. 'You must have been surprised.' She turned and smiled rather desperately. 'Frankly I'm amazed that you ever wanted to set eyes on me again.'

'You mean because of Garrett?' Claire sat down at the table, her large blue eyes very honest as they met Julia's. 'I was shocked at first, but since you never managed to bring yourself to do any harm to him after all, I don't really see why it should make any difference. You're the injured party in all this, as far as I can see.'

Julia laid a tray with painstaking care. 'Did Marcus ask you to come?'

'No. He intends coming to see you again as soon as he can. He's in the States at the moment.' Claire put out a hand and touched Julia's. 'I would have been here before, but the measles rather got in the way.'

Julia managed a smile. 'And you had two of them to contend with. I wonder you're still sane.'

'Ah,' said Claire softly, 'but I had Garrett.'

Julia moved away abruptly as the kettle boiled. Her hand shook as she poured hot water into the teapot.

'That must make quite a difference,' she agreed colourlessly.

'Julia, do you dislike Marcus?' asked Claire suddenly.

'No.'

'He said you told him to leave you alone. Was that because of your sister?'

'Yes.'

'Would you look at Marcus in a different light if you'd met in more ordinary circumstances?'

Julia picked up the tray. 'Probably. But the fact remains—Sam exists, Libby doesn't, and I just can't come to terms with the fact that Marcus is responsible for both things. In fact,' she added, on the spur of the moment, 'I'm thinking of moving away—making a fresh start somewhere else.'

Claire looked thoughtful as she followed Julia back to the sitting-room, but once in the company of Sam again was unable to make any comment, since it was obvious, even to someone who had only just made his acquaintance, that Sam understood just about everything said in his presence.

Claire stayed for half an hour, captivating Sam by her unfeigned interest in his farm and all the other toys he trotted out to show her. When she rose to go she took Julia by the hand.

'Bring Sam out to the farm when he's better,' she said.

'Farm?' said Sam, pricking up his ears.

Claire smiled at him. 'Yes, Sam. I live on a kind of farm. But we only have dogs and cats, and a guinea-pig—oh, and a rabbit. No sheep or cows, I'm afraid.'

He obviously found this a little disappointing, but graciously made it plain he'd be delighted to visit her farm just the same.

'Please come,' said Claire simply, when Julia saw her to the door.

'I don't know, Claire.' Julia sighed. 'It would only complicate things.'

'Nonsense—think how Sam would love it at Rigg Farm!'

Which was a very unfair parting shot, thought Julia, as she watched Claire's car out of sight. Up to now her whole life had been geared up to what would be best for Sam from the moment of his birth. Suddenly, violently, she wanted to do something that was best for Julia. And just exactly what she felt that was, she wasn't prepared to admit, even to herself.

CHAPTER NINE

JULIA spent the next day or two on tenterhooks, expecting a visit, or even a telephone call, from Marcus at any moment. She was disappointed. Four days went by after Claire's visit without a word from him, and since January had suddenly decided to emulate spring for an hour or two Julia took Sam out in the park for the first time, with Daisy in tow to give Laura some time to herself. Sam was jubilant at being out in the sunshine after days on end in the house, and when Julia let him out of his pushchair on the grass he tore round in circles chasing Daisy, his eyes sparkling under his knitted green cap as Julia sat on a bench watching them, shivering slightly in the cold little wind which gave the lie to January's deception. Sam was dressed in layers of wool and a warm anorak, with thick trousers and socks tucked into his rubber boots, his hands in warm woollen mittens, so Julia had no qualms about him as he and Daisy ran about with the ball. Daisy, as usual, looked like an illustration from a child's book with her blonde curls escaping from the hood of her blue coat, and Julia watched them absently, her mind far away on the problem of her future.

Her words, spoken so spontaneously to Claire about moving away, were always in her mind these days. The more she thought of it, the more it seemed the sensible thing to do. Now, while Sam was young. Perhaps she could teach again, now he was almost old enough to start nursery school. They could make a fresh start, in some place where no one had heard of Richard or Libby—or Marcus Lang.

'A penny for your thoughts,' said a familiar voice in her ear, and Julia shot to her feet, startled, to find the subject of those thoughts smiling down at her, his thick brown hair ruffled by the wind.

'Marcus!' She stared at him, thinking how different he looked in suede windbreaker and heavy tweed trousers, a roll-neck sweater in place of the formal collar and tie he normally wore.

'Mrs Murray told me where to find you, so I thought I'd come and offer you a lift home in the car.'

She glanced across the road beyond the park railings, to where the Ferrari Testarossa gleamed redly in the sunshine. 'In that? I'm sure it's not used to pushchairs and sticky children.'

'Don't be snobbish.' He grinned, then looked across to where Sam and Daisy were skipping about on the grass. 'Sam's better, I gather.'

'Yes,' said Julia stiffly, feeling absurdly awkward. 'Full of beans, in fact.'

'Which I assume poses as many problems as when he was sick.'

She nodded politely. 'Yes, indeed. By the way, thank you for sending him the farm. You really shouldn't have.'

'Why? Doesn't he like it?'

'He loves it.'

'Good.' He looked down at her wryly. 'But you'd rather not be obliged to thank me for anything, I assume!'

Which embarrassed Julia even more by reminding her that she hadn't thanked him for the flowers. She remedied the deficit formally.

'And are you going to?' Marcus asked conversationally.

She stared blankly.

'Since you received the flowers, I assume you also got the message with them,' he explained patiently.

Julia's face flooded with colour. 'I've told you it's not possible for me to work for you any longer,' she said stiffly.

'In that case let's think of something else.'

She eyed his bland face suspiciously. 'What, exactly?'

'I suggest we discuss it over dinner tonight, Julia.'

'I can't. I have Sam to think about.'

'Since the night I learned of his existence I feel *I* have Sam to think about too.' Marcus touched a finger to her cold cheek. 'Your friend Laura is only too happy to look after Sam for an hour if I take you out for a meal. She was all for the idea—said you could do with a break.'

'I'm sure she did,' said Julia, defeated.

'A very attractive lady, your friend Laura,' observed Marcus, his eyes on the children.

Julia nodded glumly, thinking of Laura as she was dressed today, in scarlet dungarees and black sweater, with her yards of hair tied up with red ribbon and her inevitable silver bangles jangling. 'Clever too. She's a very talented artist.'

'Your hair's longer now,' said Marcus, with apparent irrelevance.

'No time to get it cut.'

'Then don't. I like it like that.'

At least it was clean, thought Julia, which was a decided improvement on last time. What a pity she hadn't thought it necessary to dress a bit more elegantly for the walk in the park. Like Marcus, she was wearing a wind-cheater, but hers was ancient, of fleece-lined denim to match her Levis, and her old Western-style leather boots might be comfortable, but they were frankly scuffed, and her scrubbed face was probably pink-nosed from the cold. How nice it would be to look at least civilised for a change in Marcus's company.

'Will you?' he asked patiently.

'Will I what?'

'Have dinner with me tonight, you inattentive woman. That's the third time of asking.'

Julia nodded. 'All right. Since I seem to be outvoted two to one, what else can I say?'

He leaned against a tree, his eyes grass-green in the pale winter sunshine as he smiled mockingly at her. 'You could try sounding a little more enthusiastic!'

She was saved from reply by the arrival of two breathless children who hurled themselves at her, clutching at her with enthusiasm, and pointing to the puppy a young girl was trailing past on a lead. Suddenly Sam caught sight of Marcus and scowled, glaring up at the tall man in suspicion.

It was almost comical the way the two pairs of identical eyes stared at each other, the small boy sizing up the man with just as much attention as the man gave him in return.

'Say hello to Mr Lang, Sam,' instructed Julia, and took Daisy by the hand. 'This is Daisy, Marcus, Laura's daughter. Sam, of course, you've already met.'

Daisy smiled, and greeted the man shyly, but Sam turned truculent, refusing to say a word.

'Sam!' said Julia warningly. 'Say hello. And say thank you too. This is the kind gentleman who sent you the farm.'

Sam's eyes goggled in disbelief. '*My* farm?'

Marcus nodded. 'Did you like it?'

'Yes,' said Sam, after a prod from Julia.

'And?' said Julia, prompting. 'What do you say to Mr Lang?'

'Thank you,' said Sam reluctantly.

'Don't mention it,' said Marcus casually, then turned to the little girl. 'Would you like a ride home in my car, Daisy?' He pointed to the Ferrari. The child's eyes widened, and she looked at Julia uncertainly.

'You too, Auntie Julia?'

'Yes, of course, darling.' Julia glanced down at Sam. 'What about you, Sam? Do you want a ride in Mr Lang's car?'

Sam was so palpably torn by the instinctive hostility he felt towards 'the man', and the urgent longing he felt to ride in the Ferrari, Julia had to bite back a smile.

'You don't *have* to go in the car,' she assured him. 'You can go back in the pushchair as usual. Daisy won't mind walking back, will you, darling?'

The little girl looked crestfallen, but she shook her head bravely.

Sam, seeing the question of the car ride taken from his hands, suffered a change of heart. 'I'm cold,' he said, and coughed a little. He coughed again, harder, and Marcus picked up his cue smoothly.

'I really think you ought to go home in the car with that cough,' he said firmly. 'If you like we could go for a little ride in it before we go back to your house.'

Sam graciously agreed that this would be an excellent idea, and a few minutes later the pushchair was folded up and everyone packed into the Ferrari. Marcus drove more slowly than usual, obviously mindful of his youthful cargo, and Sam sat wide-eyed like Daisy as they left the town behind and went for a short way into the countryside before returning home. When the car was vacated, with extreme reluctance on Sam's part, Daisy thanked Marcus with the exquisite manners that seemed to come naturally to her, while Sam stood stubbing the toe of his Wellington boot on the pavement, ignoring Julia's fulminating eye.

'If you don't thank Mr Lang for taking you for a ride in his car I think he's unlikely to ask you again,' she said severely.

Sam looked up, plainly much struck by her argument. 'Thank you,' he muttered ungraciously, and touched a grubby but reverent hand to the car's gleaming red paintwork.

'A pleasure,' said Marcus gravely, his eyes dancing, then he looked at Julia. 'Eightish?' he said casually.

She flushed. 'Fine. Thank you.'

It was useless to scold Laura for her complicity, or to delude herself that she wasn't looking forward to going out for a meal, Julia decided. She was in sore need of a break from the house, from her problems, and even from Sam. In which case, she reminded herself, Marcus Lang was hardly the ideal escort for the purpose, since he was part and parcel of those same problems, especially Sam. Nevertheless Julia looked forward to the evening with an eagerness which made her full of high spirits for bathtime and playtime, even for the extra story that Sam's perspicacity told him was on the cards tonight in Julia's present mood. Happily, thanks to all the running about in the fresh air, followed by the excitement of the car-ride, Sam was fast asleep before the end of the obligatory performance of *The Owl and the Pussy-Cat*, and Julia was left with enough time on her hands to go through her wardrobe to decide what to wear.

Not that she needed very much time for that particular exercise, she thought gloomily. It was too cold for the pink crêpe, she had no desire to wear the red skirt and shirt bought for the Christmas dance, and in the end fell back on a plain black velvet dress she had pushed to one side a couple of years before as being too short. Now that hemlines were a matter of taste rather than fashion Julia decided the dress would do. She hesitated about wearing the beautiful string of pearls Marcus had given her, but they added such a new dimension to the stark little dress that she couldn't resist them, and felt moderately pleased with her reflection as she sprayed herself with the last of her precious perfume. She put on the black cotton trenchcoat bought while she was still earning a generous salary at Lang's, added the scarlet scarf Sue had given her for Christmas, and was chatting idly to Laura when a very quiet knock on the front door heralded Marcus's arrival.

'Enjoy yourself,' ordered Laura trenchantly. 'Eat, drink and do your darnedest to be merry, Julia. Orders!'

Julia laughed, and opened the door to Marcus, whispering her goodbyes as she hurried him back down the path to the gate.

'Sorry I couldn't ask you in, but Sam might wake if he heard you and then we'd never get off.'

'That's why I didn't ring the bell.' When Marcus helped her into the Ferrari he arranged a thick, soft rug over her knees. 'It's colder tonight,' he said as he got in beside her. 'I felt a few flakes of snow as I came out of the house, but the forecast said wintry showers, so I think we'll chance a trip out into the country, as planned.' He glanced at her as he switched on the ignition. 'Are you warm enough? You should have brought a heavier coat.'

Julia agreed, shivering, and huddled gratefully under the rug.

'I thought we'd go into the Cotswolds and eat big platefuls of rare roast beef in front of a roaring fire,' he said as they left the town.

'Sounds wonderful,' said Julia. And so it was. The old coaching inn Marcus drove her to was a fair distance away from Pennington, but worth the journey when they arrived. The building looked like something on a picture postcard, and the promised roaring fire, in both bar and dining-room, set the mood for the entire evening, which was more relaxed and enjoyable than Julia would have believed possible beforehand. As she ate buttered crab, followed by the promised roast beef, which was carved by a genial chef at the table, Julia decided her problems could have a night off. She was enjoying herself. And so, to her rather gratified surprise, was Marcus.

He gave her an entertaining account of his trip to the United States, brought her up to date on the latest sins of his now fully-recovered nephews, discussed a new computer he was about to put on the market, told her about a Tennessee Williams play he'd enjoyed at the National Theatre not long before, thereby satisfying Julia's conversation-starved soul to such a degree she felt bound to thank him for it.

'You mean you have something you really are grateful for as far as I'm concerned?' he said, amused.

Julia finished her wine appreciatively. 'Mm, lovely. And if all you'd had since Christmas was a sick baby boy for company you'd be glad for some adult conversation too. Not that I'm decrying Laura,' she added hastily, 'but our sessions together tend to be brief, since we more or less mind each other's child all the time so the other one can do her own thing. And since Sam's measles even that hasn't been possible. In fact the only other person I've had a conversation with is

Claire——' She stopped short at the look on Marcus's face.

'Claire came to see you?' he said, thunderstruck.

'I gather you told her about Sam.'

'I did. But it never occurred to me she'd come to see for herself.'

'Sam was excessively taken with her,' said Julia.

'Which is more than can be said for his feelings towards me!' Marcus refilled her wine-glass, his smile a little twisted.

'I think he may have softened now he knows you're the one who gave him his farm, not to mention being the owner of the red car.' Julia smiled. 'Sam obviously considers you a man of taste, despite his innate feelings of hostility towards you.'

'Our first meeting was hardly satisfactory by film and fiction standards,' said Marcus drily.

'You mean he didn't beam at you and lisp "Daddy" as he hurled himself into your arms!' Julia grinned. 'He's hostile towards you because he's jealous, Marcus. He's not used to seeing me pay attention to any male except him.'

Marcus leaned forward slightly, capturing her hand. 'Do *you* feel hostile towards me, Julia?'

Her lashes instantly dropped to veil her eyes. 'No, not really,' she said, hoping very much he was unable to tell how different her feelings at this moment actually were. She scoffed at herself. A ride in a car, an expensive dinner and a little sweet-talk, and here she was, ready to melt like butter in this large, contained man's hands. Only he hadn't been quite so contained the other night, she reminded herself, brightening.

'I'd give a lot to know what's going on under that shiny black mop of yours,' he said huskily, then moved away quickly as the waiter appeared with their coffee.

By the time Julia had filled their cups, and refused offers of brandy, she had herself more in hand. 'You brought me out tonight to discuss something,' she reminded him. 'It's almost time to go home and you haven't even started yet.'

Marcus asked her permission to smoke a cigar, and when it was lit and he was looking at her through a haze of blue, expensive smoke he said abruptly,

'How do you think of me now, Julia?'

'Right now?'

'No. I mean since you've learned the truth about Sam.'

'You mean do I feel you're responsible for Libby's death.'

He winced, and took a sip of the brandy in his glass. 'That's a terrible crime to burden me with for the rest of my life, Julia. Lord knows I'd give much to undo what happened, but since I can't make any reparation to your sister, I've brought you here tonight to ask if you'll allow me to make my reparation to the son I never knew I had until now.'

'Reparation,' said Julia thoughtfully. 'A Biblical ring about it, isn't there?'

'Right up your street, then. Wasn't your whole motivation on the lines of "an eye for an eye", and so on, when you set out to bring Garrett's world down round his ears?'

She shuddered. 'Very true. But I just didn't have the bottle, when it came to the push.' She smiled at him suddenly. 'For which, in the light of recent revelations, I am profoundly thankful. My lack of courage saved a great deal of grief and misery in the long run, didn't it?'

'Except that I'm now very much minus my super-efficient Mrs North.' His eyes, dark in the soft candlelight of their secluded corner, held hers very deliberately. 'And she tells me she won't come back to me.'

'And she meant it.'

'Would you come back to me in another capacity?' he said softly.

Julia eyed him suspiciously. 'Clarify, please.'

He leaned back, relaxed. 'Well, put it like this. After Nicola decided I wasn't suitable husband material I more or less abandoned the whole idea of marriage. I felt that if Lang Holdings needed more Langs to carry on the name Garrett's boys would fill the bill nicely, leaving me to the freedom and privileges of bachelorhood. I'd never hankered after babies, to be honest, not exactly keen on all the nappies and broken nights and restrictions that come as part of the package. I never felt the need of a son in my image and all that. Then I find that, quite by accident, I *do* have a son.'

'Housebroken too,' murmured Julia.

'Don't be flippant. What I'm trying to say is that I'd like to adopt Sam.'

Julia's eyes opened wide. 'Adopt Sam? Take him away from me?'

'No. To adopt Sam I need a wife. I don't have one any more. And you don't have a husband any more. Doesn't all this sound like an equation with a very simple solution?'

'Did you run it through on the computer, or something?' Julia shook her head in wonder. 'These are people you're talking about, Marcus, not a set of statistics!'

'I'm asking you to marry me,' said Marcus with a slow deliberation which left her in no doubt that he was in deadly earnest. 'Come back to me, Julia, as a wife.

Then Sam would have two parents, and you'd have a home and a life-style which would take that look of desperate anxiety from your eyes, allow you to be a girl again. Because that's all you are, despite all this shellacked efficiency you coat yourself with, Julia.' He leaned forward and took her hand again. 'Would it be so unthinkable to be married to me? You know me well enough, my sins of omission and commission, the way I like my coffee.' He smiled persuasively into her watchful eyes.

'Sam doesn't like you very much,' she said, thinking fast.

'Sam's young enough to learn. It's of more importance to me to learn whether *you* like me.'

'Do you like *me*?'

He looked squarely into her eyes. There was a momentary flicker in their depths before he smiled very wryly indeed, and tightened his clasp on her hand.

'Oh, yes, Julia. I like you.'

'Even though I schemed and plotted my way into your life?'

'Since otherwise I'm unlikely to have met you, I'm very grateful you did!'

'Would you want more children?' she asked bluntly.

He blinked. 'You don't believe in wrapping things up, do you? But to answer you in kind, I really have no preference. If you don't want any, that's all right by me. I'd still have Sam from the same stock, so to speak.'

'Not exactly. Sam and I are not blood relations. I don't even know what my real pedigree is. I could be anybody,' Julia reminded him.

'Of course, I'd forgotten that.' Marcus raised her hand to his lips and kissed it with a fervour and such unexpected grace that tears thickened her throat. 'Not that it matters, Julia. Who and what you are is written in your face, and borne out by your conduct. Whoever your parents were, they have every right to be proud of their daughter.'

At which the tears she'd been swallowing grew unruly, and one or two of them rolled down Julia's cheeks, making her heartily glad the dining-room was deserted by this time. Marcus leaned forward and touched his damask napkin to them, then rose to his feet.

'Shall we go?'

He helped her into the black cotton trenchcoat as if it were rarest mink, then paid the bill while she retreated to the cloakroom to make repairs. To her surprise when she joined him at the front entrance she found the world outside was a white wilderness. Marcus gave a quick look at her suede shoes and picked her up in his arms to cover the short distance to the Ferrari. If only he knew it, the feel of his arms holding me safe is more persuasion than any words could be, thought Julia, as he carefully deposited her in the low seat of the car.

'We'd better get going. This looks nasty,' he said, peering through the whirling white flakes. 'I'd never have come so far out if I'd thought the weather would worsen like this.'

'But it was so beautiful this afternoon,' said Julia, and rubbed a place clear on the side window as Marcus backed carefully from the parking space.

'I was a fool to risk it,' he said tightly, as they turned on to a road already thick with snow. 'It's almost impassable already. It must have snowed like hell all evening. The main roads are probably clear enough, but we have several very country miles to negotiate until we reach one of them. The Range Rover's in for a service, otherwise I'd never have brought the damn Ferrari.'

After a while it became clear that they were likely to run into difficulties if they went much further. Julia could feel the tension in Marcus as he peered through the windscreen.

'It's no good, Julia, we'll just have to turn back. It's a steep, twisting stretch from here on, and I don't fancy it, frankly. If I make it back to the inn at least we'll probably get a couple of rooms for the night.'

'Stay the night!' Julia stared at him in dismay. 'But Marcus, what about Sam?'

'If you ring Laura from the hotel and tell her what's happened I'm sure she'll be happy to look after Sam until I can get you back there in the morning.' Marcus peered at his watch. 'Garrett's away in Birmingham, otherwise I'd get him to come and rescue us.'

Julia thought it best not to argue, because on the short journey back to the inn Marcus needed all his attention to avoid getting stuck in the snow which was blanketing out the narrow road with alarming rapidity. She was heartily glad when the welcoming lights of the isolated hotel came into view.

'If they don't have a room perhaps they'll let us sit by that fire in the hotel lounge,' she said philosophically, and Marcus grinned at her as he switched off the ignition with a sigh of relief.

'Thank you, Julia.'

'For what?'

'For not making a fuss.'

'Not much point, really,' she said prosaically. 'The snow isn't your fault.'

'I'm glad something isn't.' Marcus reached into the back of the car for a sheepskin jacket and shrugged into it with some difficulty in the confines of the low-slung car. He opened the door into the howling wind, and slammed it quickly before dodging round to Julia's side. He scooped her out of the car, ramming the door shut with his knee, then bore her off through the blizzard as rapidly as possible, gasping with the effort as he set her on her feet in the lobby of the hotel. 'Phew!' he said breathlessly. 'Thank goodness for that. Are you all right?'

Apart from the cold, and the snowflakes melting on her hair, Julia felt fine, and told him so, as the sympathetic hotel owner came forward to offer assistance.

The accommodation at the small hotel was limited, and since some of the earlier diners had also decided to avail themselves of its hospitality there was only one room left to offer them, said the man apologetically. The room was their largest, and the best in the hotel, but the fact remained, it would have to be shared.

'Does it have any furniture besides a bed?' asked Marcus, and Julia felt her colour rise as the manager assured them the bedroom contained a sofa, and offered to provide extra bedding if the gentleman wished to sleep on it. Marcus turned to Julia, his face carefully expressionless. 'Apparently they lock the public rooms at night, and quite obviously don't fancy having me sleep down here, so are you willing to share just this once?' The proprietor had moved tactfully out of earshot, and Marcus added quietly, 'You need have no fear I'll take advantage of the situation, Julia.' He smiled a little. 'And I don't believe I snore.'

'In that case, how can I refuse?' she said lightly, and went to ring Laura. Laura was surprised, amused, and said a few encouraging things Julia was heartily glad Marcus couldn't hear.

'I'm sorry about this, Laura. I had no idea we'd get stuck in a howling blizzard.'

'Better to stay where you are rather than risk getting marooned miles from anywhere, love. Goodnight—and pleasant dreams,' said Laura slyly.

The proprietor had not misled them about the quality of the room. It was larger than expected, with beams on the low ceiling, a stone-cowled fireplace, latticed windows, a sofa and two chairs, various antique chests and tables, and a four-poster bed which they were told Charles the Second was reputed to have slept in.

'Not Queen Elizabeth?' murmured Marcus when they were alone, and suddenly Julia's sense of humour returned.

'*She* took her own bath everywhere with her—let's hope they have something more contemporary here!'

The adjoining bathroom was everything that could be wished for, and Marcus advised Julia to take a hot shower before she got into the imposing bed. 'You look frozen,' he said, and smiled. 'I'll dash downstairs to the bar and see if mine host can provide some coffee and brandy while you get yourself sorted out.'

Julia was deeply grateful for his tact, and had a blissfully hot but very swift bath before diving into the bed, attired in the satin slip worn beneath her dress. The anachronistic electric over-blanket was a welcome surprise, and she snuggled down gratefully, surprised to feel less awkward about the situation than she had anticipated.

Marcus left a tactful interval before his knock signalled his return. He came into the room bearing a tray with coffee and a brandy decanter. 'They wanted to have it sent up,' he said, smiling. 'But I thought you'd prefer my personal brand of room service in the circumstances.'

'Very true,' said Julia, and smiled back. 'This sort of thing is rather outside my experience.'

'Don't worry, Julia,' he said cheerfully. 'Morning will soon be here, and I'll have you home safe and sound before you know it.'

He was friendly and impersonal, talking about everything under the sun while he poured coffee and propped pillows behind her so she could drink it. He insisted she follow the coffee with a generous measure of brandy, and though she disliked the taste of the spirit for once she decided it might be the sensible thing to do in the circumstances. Marcus switched off her blanket and she slid under the covers into a cocoon of warmth, her eyes growing heavy as he went off to the bathroom to prepare for the night.

A small, rose-shaded lamp on the dressing-table cast a faint glow over the room as he came quietly back into the bedroom swathed in a bath towel. Julia watched drowsily as he piled blankets on the sofa, which was hard and high-backed, and designed for two people to sit on, and to sit upright at that. She giggled to herself as she saw his large frame contorting itself in various positions aimed at adapting itself to the sofa's proportions as he wrapped the blankets around him. Several smothered curses added to her amusement. Marcus was obviously having severe difficulties with his improvised resting-place. She fell asleep to the accompaniment of restless thrashings from her room-mate, her last thoughts of Sam, and whether he would wake and make trouble for Laura when he found his 'Mummy' was missing.

She surfaced unwillingly from a deep sleep to the sound of her name whispered urgently in her ear.

'Wh-what's the matter?' she said thickly. 'Sam?'

'No, me. I'm bloody well freezing,' said Marcus, his teeth chattering. 'Will you yell blue murder if I get in the bed with you? I promise I'll stay on my side.'

Julia yawned, too sleepy to bother about proprieties. 'Oh, all right. But keep quiet—I'm tired.'

There was a heartfelt sigh of relief from Marcus as he slid into the bed. She felt the mattress depress with the weight of his body, the vibration as he lay shivering in the darkness, but none of it was enough to stop her sliding back into oblivion, all her scruples vanquished by the sheer basic need for sleep.

She woke again to a room she thought must be lit by the cold light of dawn, then she saw stars through the lattice and realised it was the reflection of the snow outside which gave an impression of luminosity. At the sound of deep breathing beside her she turned her head sharply, but Marcus lay with his back turned to her, as near the far edge of the bed as he could get, just as he'd promised. She smiled to herself in the half-dark. How organised he was, even in his sleep. He'd promised to keep away from her and there he was, neatly arranged so that not even an erring toe could come into contact with hers. She stared up into the darkness of the bed's canopy. It was a long time since she'd shared a bed with a man. Richard had slept as close to her as he could get, coiling his arms and legs round her in possession even in his sleep. It had irritated her sometimes. Then, after their pitifully brief time together, less than six months all told, she had missed having him near, missed having someone to hold her in the night.

What a strange situation this is, she thought, wondering what time it was, and sat up very gingerly to peer at the luminous dial of Marcus's watch on his outflung arm. Two o'clock. A lot of night to go yet. She eased herself back down and tried to get back to sleep, but the first weariness had gone. She felt restless and wakeful, and deeply conscious, now, of the sleeping form beside her. And after a while, though he hadn't moved a muscle, she could tell Marcus was awake too. She lay like a statue, hardly daring to breathe, but he was undeceived.

'Julia?' he whispered. 'Did I disturb you?'

'No. I think the light from the snow woke me. I thought it was morning.' She felt a slight rustle as he looked at his watch.

'A long time to go until then. Are you cold?'

The moment he mentioned it Julia realised she was very cold indeed, and that it was probably the temperature drop which had woken her up.

'Will you black my eye if I move closer?' he asked meekly. 'If we huddle together our combined body heat will warm us up very quickly.'

Julia didn't doubt it for a moment. She bit her lip, undecided. 'Do you mind if I ask you a question?'

He let out a snort of laughter. 'No. What is it?'

She took in as deep a breath as her suddenly chattering teeth would allow. 'Are you wearing any clothes, Marcus?'

CHAPTER TEN

MARCUS lay shaking with laughter in the darkness. 'Isn't it a bit late to ask that now? But since it's so important, yes, Julia, I'm wearing a rather smart pair of black and white boxer shorts. A pity really. Last night I'd have sold my soul for red flannel pyjamas.'

Julia giggled involuntarily. Marcus Lang and red flannel sounded like strange bedfellows. She sobered. No stranger bedfellows, now she came to think of it, than Marcus Lang and Julia North. If she'd thought for a moment the evening would end like this she'd have done better to stay safely at home.

'Do I take it you're weighing up the pros and cons of togetherness?' he asked plaintively. 'Or shall we just lie here several inches apart and shiver for the rest of the night?'

'Why not just turn on the electric blanket?' suggested Julia.

'Because I'd much rather cuddle up to you,' he said, and did so with the air of a man prepared to brook no opposition. He settled her in the curve of his body, her back to him, spoon-fashion, his chin on her hair and his arm holding her close around her waist. 'There,' he whispered in her ear. 'Not so bad, is it?'

Not so bad was an understatement. To Julia the haven of Marcus Lang's arms was a ravishing experience. It was wonderful to feel safe and warm and cherished, with no hint of anything but comfort in the way he held her. Not impersonally, exactly, she decided. Being held close to a man's half-clothed body could never be altogether impersonal.

'It's fine,' she said a little breathlessly. 'Goodnight, Marcus'

'Goodnight, Julia.'

She felt his lips on her hair, and lay very still, luxuriating in the warmth and protection of his arms. The feeling of bliss lasted for several minutes, then changed. Neither of them had moved, apart from the necessity of merely breathing. Nevertheless, something was different. The posture of Marcus's body was no longer relaxed. Julia could feel the tension in his muscles. It communicated itself to her own, and her mouth dried. It suddenly became imperative to return to her own half of the bed, but she was wary of making the first move, afraid it might be misinterpreted.

'Perhaps this wasn't such a good idea after all,' said Marcus hoarsely. 'I was genuinely cold before, I assure you, but now I rather fancy if someone struck a match I'd go up in flames.'

Julia tensed as she felt a hard stirring against her which made it only too clear he meant what he said. She shifted away quickly, but his arm shot out to haul her back.

'Don't go away,' he whispered. 'Come back to me.'

'No—Marcus, please.' She began to breathe in quick, frightened gasps. 'I told you I didn't——'

'I know. But this is different. I want you to be my wife, Julia. I want you like this all the time, right where you are now. For always.'

Julia pushed at him wildly. 'No, you don't. You're just like any other man in the heat of the moment, using persuasion to get what you want.'

He growled deep in his throat and pulled her beneath him. 'Oh no, I'm not. Unlike "other men", I don't need

to. You forget, I've got a fancy car and enough money
to ensure a woman's favours any time without saying a
word, Julia.'

She fought free, her voice low and shaken with affront. 'Then make love to one of those women. I'm not
open to offers.'

'I haven't made love to anyone at all since I first laid
eyes on you,' he said unevenly. 'For heaven's sake, Julia,
let me love you. Please! Or do you want to hear me beg?
I will if you want.'

Julia lay very still. 'How do I know you don't still
love Nicola?' she said flatly.

'Because once I met you I realised she was no longer
necessary to me,' he said, and turned over on his back.

'And how do I know someone else wouldn't replace
me—if—if——'

'If you let me share your life?' Very carefully he drew
her against him. 'Because once you belong to me I'll do
my best to make you want to stay with me, Julia. We've
both been married before. We know that nothing is
guaranteed forever. But I promise you I'll cherish you
for the rest of your life, do my best to make you happy.'

'Will you still feel like that if I won't let you make
love to me now, if I insist on making this night a kind
of test of your intentions towards me?'

Marcus gave a great, shuddering sigh. 'Yes, I'll even
do that. I shall lie here like an effigy on a tomb for the
rest of the night, and pray they serve breakfast at the
crack of dawn in this establishment. You are one cruel
lady, Julia North.'

Julia smiled in the darkness. 'Would you feel happier
if I told you the cruelty worked both ways?'

'What do you mean?'

'To be honest, I would—would very much like you to make love to me. But I'd like to be clear about your motives. Is it just sheer propinquity? Or do you mean what you say about wanting Sam and me to live with you?'

There was a very pregnant pause. Marcus cleared his throat. 'Julia, I might just manage to lie here virtuously if I believed I was the only one tortured by carnal longings. But if you're actually saying you're condemning *both* of us to frustration I'm off back to that hellish sofa. Its springs are at least likely to divert my weak male flesh from the other sensations gnawing at it.'

And Marcus heaved himself out of bed and sprinted for the pile of blankets on the sofa, leaving her alone and deflated in the middle of the four-poster bed. She lay battling with feelings she had forgotten. In fact, she decided, since the feelings were mainly frustration they were probably entirely new, since Richard had always been more eager for lovemaking than she during their time together. Why did she always have to make everything so difficult for herself? she thought bitterly. Why couldn't she just have let Marcus make love to her? She had let him into the bed, she reminded herself. Any man would be entitled to take that as some kind of go-ahead in the circumstances. She listened to his vain attempts to get comfortable on the much-maligned sofa and came to a decision.

'Marcus?' she said softly.

'Well?' His tone was discouraging.

'I'm sorry.'

Silence.

'What,' he said at last, 'do you mean, precisely?'

Julia wriggled to the edge of the bed and swung her feet to the floor, shivering as she held out her arms to him in appeal. 'To quote a—a very dear friend of mine, come back to me. Please.'

Almost in one movement Marcus leapt from the sofa, scooped her up in his arms and slid back under the covers with her body held as close to his as was humanly possible, his mouth on hers.

'What changed your mind?' he demanded, in between raining kisses all over her cold face.

'I was cold,' she said with difficulty, her face beginning to glow, not only with warmth but with a mounting delight.

'I don't think you're cold at all,' he said caressingly.

'I'm not. Now.' She gasped as he ran his mouth down her throat to her breasts. 'Marcus——'

'Mm?' he said inattentively.

'This doesn't mean you're *bound* to anything.'

'Be quiet, you stupid girl!'

'You're rude.'

'You're delicious.'

'Ouch—you bit me!'

'No, I didn't. I just nipped.' He laughed breathlessly, and Julia laughed with him, suddenly finding it all such wonderful fun. Marcus was playing with her, and she loved it. He tickled and teased, and she pinched him in retaliation, and he shook her and kissed her and caressed her until she wasn't laughing any more. She heard herself plead and Marcus laugh in a very different way, deep in his throat in triumph, and she shivered as his hands drew responses from her she knew quite well she had never felt before. The playing was over and the loving had begun, and she surrendered herself to him with a generosity that made him gasp and murmur things in her ear that sent waves of heat through her body until she found it impossible to believe she had ever been cold, or ever would be again.

And when it was no longer possible to exist apart they came together with such passionate exactitude it seemed each had been fashioned solely for the other, already tuned to each other's rhythms so perfectly they achieved a degree of mutual ecstasy totally outside Julia's limited experience.

Afterwards Julia fell deeply asleep held close in Marcus's arms, and woke in the morning with a start to the sound of an ominous rumble and then a muffled thud outside. She slid out of bed, pulling on her trenchcoat as she peered down through the window at the scene outside in the courtyard. Several men, including the proprietor of the hotel, were making their way with difficulty to a great mound of snow below Julia's window. She put a hand to her mouth, suddenly realising that the Ferrari was nowhere in sight, which meant it could only be buried under the miniature avalanche of snow which the rise in temperature had sent sliding from the roof of the hotel to the car park below.

She flew over to the bed and urgently shook Marcus awake. He sat up, blinking and yawning, as he ran a hand over his dark-stubbled jaw.

'Marcus—quickly!' she repeated. 'A pile of snow just fell off the roof and buried the Ferrari.'

His reaction was almost comic. With a violent curse he leapt from the bed without a thought for his nudity, and ran to the window to stare down at the figures frantically digging in the courtyard. Fuming, he threw on his clothes and tore from from the room without a word to Julia.

Not even a backward glance, she thought glumly. So much for romance! No tender words or a wake-up kiss, just a string of curses and all his attention on his beloved car. While he was gone she washed and dressed, doing the best she could with only a lipstick and comb, feeling faintly disreputable in black velvet and pearls so early in the day. She put the pearls in her handbag, tidied the pile of blankets on the sofa, and without much success tried to make the bed look as if she'd slept in it alone. The she laughed at herself. What did it matter? No one would believe she'd shared a room with Marcus without sharing the bed, anyway. And they were right. She belted on the trenchcoat, glad of the red wool scarf she had worn last night. She tucked it into her collar, then stood irresolute, wondering whether to go downstairs, or just stay where she was and wait for Marcus to come back.

A knock at the door solved the problem. A young girl came in with a tray of coffee, explaining that the owner's wife had sent it, thinking Julia might be cold.

'The electricity's off, so I'm afraid there's no heating in the rooms,' said the girl apologetically. 'Luckily we've got an Aga in the kitchen, so at least you can have a hot drink.'

Julia thanked her, and sat down on the sofa, tucking one of the blankets round her as she sipped gratefully.

Marcus strode back into the room with a face like thunder.

'Much damage to the car?' asked Julia, getting up to pour him a cup of coffee.

'The snow landed smack on the Ferrari's roof. There's a bloody great dent in it,' he said bitterly.

'Oh, bad luck! Will it mean much repair work?'

He swallowed the coffee, then went into the bathroom, shouting through the door as he washed. 'A small fortune, at a rough guess.'

'Won't the insurance cover it?'

'Shouldn't think so. I'm pretty sure this type of accident comes under the heading "Act of God" as far as insurance companies are concerned.'

Julia looked at her watch anxiously. 'By the way, does this mean you can't drive the car back to Pennington?'

Marcus came out of the bathroom and shrugged on his sheepskin jacket. 'Couldn't anyway—the roads aren't clear enough. Don't worry, the owner says a farmer down the road will take us in his Land Rover. The garage can collect the Ferrari when the snow's cleared.'

'Oh, good,' said Julia brightly, bitterly sorry now she'd ever consented to dine with Marcus at all, let alone sleep with him. This morning they might have been strangers. And all over a stupid phallic symbol of a car! 'How soon can we be off, then?'

'As soon as the man arrives, I suppose.' Marcus looked at her sharply, apparently seeing her clearly for the first time. 'You all right, Julia?'

'Of course.' She smiled politely. 'Just anxious to get back to Sam.'

He frowned. 'You seem very distant.'

She was distant! She bit back an angry retort. 'I'm not very good in the mornings. Besides,' she added, looking him straight in the eye, 'the morning after doesn't necessarily have a great deal to do with the night before, does it?'

Marcus's face went rigid. 'Ah! I see. We just pretend last night never happened.'

'Something like that——' Julia turned, relieved, as the same girl tapped on the door and popped her head round it.

'Bert Weekes is here in the Land Rover, Mr Lang.'

'Thank you.' Marcus smiled at the girl absently. 'We'll be down in a moment.'

As the door closed he turned back to Julia with a look that made her quail. 'It was not my intention to end up sharing a bed when I asked you to dine with me yesterday, Julia. I wield a fair amount of influence in my professional life, it's true, but so far I've failed to extend it as far as controlling the weather.'

'Of course not. I'm not blaming you, Marcus. For anything.' Julia picked up her gloves and drew them on with an air of finality, pride goading her on to hurt him as he was hurting her. 'Like the insurance company, we'll think of last night as an act of God, of no importance whatsoever. Now I think we'd better be on our way.'

The silence between them was tangible as they went downstairs and thanked their host for all his kindness. As Marcus settled their bill Julia busied herself by reading a framed history of the building on a wall near the reception desk, not sure whether she was sorry or grateful someone would be with them on the way home to prevent any private conversation.

'Hello, Mrs North,' said a surprised voice behind her. 'Fancy meeting you here!'

She turned sharply, trying to hide her horror as she came face to face with someone she recognised with despair. Not again! Dennis Hall, of the marketing department of Lang Holdings, stood smiling at her.

'Why, Dennis. Hello,' she said, doing her best to smile back.

'Don't tell me you got marooned here too!' The cheerful young man laughed, and jerked his head towards two other young men coming down the stairs. 'The three of us came back this way from Oxford last night and decided it wasn't on trying to get any further. Hope the roads are passable this morning. Don't fancy being late, we're due in a meeting with the big white chief...'

At any other time Julia would have found the utter dismay on Dennis Hall's face amusing as he caught sight of Marcus. But for the moment all she could think of was the sheer embarrassment of the situation. Marcus appeared not in the least put out, and made no attempt to explain his presence at the hotel with Julia. He merely joked with his three uneasy employees about the coincidence, then took Julia's arm and hurried her out to the waiting Land Rover.

Since it wasn't possible to discuss the incident on the way back in the presence of the jovial Mr Weekes, Julia sat in silence while Marcus chatted with the farmer. Profoundly thankful when the vehicle drew up outside the house in Chester Road, she thanked their rescuer, said a polite goodbye to Marcus without looking at him, and ran up the path before he could do anything to prevent her.

Laura was waiting for her in the sitting-room with a tearful Sam in her arms. She handed over the little boy, smiling as the child threw his arms convulsively around Julia's neck.

'I'm afraid he was a bit thrown this morning when he woke to find me instead of you.'

Julia soothed Sam's tearful scolding, and stroked his hair as she smiled ruefully at Laura. 'I'm sorry about last night, Laura.'

'Are you?' said the other girl shrewdly.

She nodded. 'Definitely one of those events I'd rather hadn't happened.'

'What *did* happen? I was watching from the window when you arrived. Did the Ferrari turn into a muddy old Land Rover on the stroke of midnight?'

'If it had I could have come home!' Julia gave an expurgated version of the evening, finishing up with the embarrassing encounter with three of Marcus Lang's bright young marketing men. 'It made it all so grubby-feeling, somehow,' she finished despondently.

'What does it matter, if your conscience is clear?' Laura's eyes narrowed as she watched Julia bury her scarlet face in Sam's curls. 'Oh, I see. You slept with him.'

'Yes.'

'And?'

'What do you mean, "and"?'

'So what happens now?'

With reluctance Julia mentioned Marcus's plans for their future.

'So all's well that ends well,' said Laura promptly. 'After all, he is Sam's——' She stopped, conscious of Sam's sudden interest.

'I know. That's what bothers me. I can't rid myself of the feeling that his motives are all mixed up with guilt about Libby, not to mention the owner of sharp little ears.'

'Oh, Julia, what does it matter? Is he a good lover?'

'Laura!' Julia's eyes almost popped out, then she began to laugh. 'You're incorrigible!'

'No—just practical.' Laura led the way into the kitchen and made coffee, while Julia sat down with Sam cuddled close against her shoulder. 'As I see it Marcus Lang is very comfortably off, and from the look of your face just now I'd bet my boots he's pretty accomplished in bed, *and* he also has this other very strong claim we can't mention in front of *le petit garçon* here.'

'So you think I should forget about Libby and make the most of a chance I'm never likely to get in my life again?'

Laura moved close, and with a very rare caress touched Julia's cheek. 'I think you should do what you really and truly *want* to do, love. Never mind what happened in the past. Just think about the present and the future, and follow your instincts. If they tell you to go it alone, fine. If they don't, you know what to do about that too. Don't you?' she added deliberately, and left Julia alone with Sam and her thoughts for company, neither of which made for a very restful day, particularly as Julia fully expected a call from Marcus at any minute.

She had to force herself to take Sam and Daisy out for a walk to the snowy park, not wanting to be out if Marcus rang. Her disappointment when she found he hadn't was so intense she was angry with herself. After all, she told herself stringently, she had only herself to blame. She had been the one to dismiss their night together as a mere commonplace happening to forget about next day. Yet all she'd wanted was for Marcus to hold her in his arms and tell her again that he wanted her, reassure her that her surrender of the night was not a thing he held cheap. Instead he had gone tearing off to help dig out the Ferrari, and Julia had a nagging suspicion she had behaved rather like Sam in a fit of sulks afterwards.

When several days passed without a word she gradually began to resign herself to the fact that Marcus Lang was history. It was over. Secretly she had hoped against hope that their lovemaking might have resulted in a child, but nature soon disabused her of that idea. One way and another it was only natural to feel depressed, she told herself firmly, and began to turn her attention in earnest to the matter of finding a job. When, to her infinite relief, she was asked to attend a firm of solicitors for interview for a part-time secretarial job, she went off dressed in her smartest office clothes, her spirits higher than they had been for some time.

Her spirits were uplifted even further when the elderly solicitor who interviewed her offered her the post on the spot. Subject, of course, he said kindly, to a reference from her previous employer. Julia furnished him with Marcus's address and telephone number, and assured Mr Hetherington she would be delighted to start the following Monday.

To her fury she received an apologetic letter from Hetherington and Dunn a day or two later regretting that, as the necessary reference had not been forthcoming from Mr Lang, and since the nature of their work was so highly confidential, they were sure Mrs North would understand why they were unable to offer her the job after all.

Julia dialled the number of Lang Holdings with a hand that shook with rage.

'Rowena?' she said, when the receptionist answered. 'Julia North here. Yes, yes, I'm much better, thanks. Is Mr Lang available?'

Mr Lang, she was told, was not only unavailable, he was in Germany. He would be back that evening, added Rowena helpfully, and offered to take a message.

Since the message she had for Marcus would have shocked Rowena to the core, Julia thanked the receptionist and declined, saying she would ring Mr Lang some other time.

Fuming and frustrated, Julia's mind went round in circles as she wondered why her reference had been refused. The mere thought of it was so mortifying she paced up and down her small sitting-room like an angry tigress, until Sam voiced his objections indignantly, complaining that she was blocking his view of his favourite lunchtime programme on the television.

She would ring Marcus at home tonight, Julia decided, find out what the hell he was playing at. What right had he to make life so impossible for her? If he refused a reference to anyone who cared to employ her, how did he imagine she was to earn a living?

From Miss Pennycook Julia had learned that when Marcus and Nicola Lang were divorced he had sold their Georgian town house, and bought a country property near his brother's place. Julia had never been there but had often had occasion to ring Marcus when he was at home. She waited until Sam was asleep that evening, then dialled the number, drumming her fingers impatiently as she listened to it ringing. There was no answer. Out on the town, probably, she thought, her mouth tightening. On impulse she rang Claire's number. Garrett's friendly voice greeted her with surprise when she announced herself.

'Julia! We've been very concerned about you. How are you? Claire's badly wanted to get in touch, but Marcus told us you'd given him his marching orders, and on no account were we to interfere.'

Julia's heart sank down to her black leather boots. 'Oh, I see. I'm fine, actually, Garrett, but I just wanted a word with Marcus. I rang his house a minute ago, but there was no answer, so I thought he might be with you.'

Garrett sounded worried. 'He should have been home by this time, but his flight into Heathrow's been delayed. Most of the Continent is blanketed in this freezing fog we've got here, apparently.'

Julia stood very still. 'You mean he's held up at a German airport?'

There was silence on the line for a moment. 'Actually, no,' said Garrett with reluctance. 'His driver rang from Heathrow a short while ago. Apparently the plane took off from Lohausen airport in Dusseldorf only half an hour behind schedule. It should have landed at Heathrow long since.'

Julia swallowed. 'Probably held up a bit in the fog, then,' she said with an effort.

'Look,' said Garrett quickly, 'as soon as he arrives home I'll tell him to ring you——'

'Oh, no,' said Julia, appalled. 'Please, don't do that. It's nothing important.'

'Anything that's likely to improve Marcus's present mood is important, Julia,' said Garrett emphatically. 'To all of us. He's been like a bear with a sore head lately.'

Julia's anxiety was only slightly tempered by this piece of news. 'I don't imagine that's anything to do with me. Anyway, I must go. Thank you, Garrett. Give my love to Claire.'

'Are you worried about Marcus?' asked Garrett bluntly.

'I'd be worried about anyone in the same circumstances. I—I hope you have news of him soon.'

'So do I,' said Garrett with feeling. 'At the risk of sounding mawkish, I'm hellishly fond of my big brother, you know.'

So was she, thought Julia bleakly, and bade Garrett goodbye, wishing afterwards she'd let him tell Marcus to ring her the moment he was home. If he ever came home. Her blood froze at the thought, and she stood like a statue in the narrow hall. Not again, surely! One by one everyone she had ever cared for had been taken away from her: her parents, Richard, Libby. Sam was all she had left. It was like a physical pain to think she might never see Marcus again when they had parted on such hostile terms. She winced at her own vanity in thinking he would never leave things as they were when they parted that morning, sure he would take no notice of her stupid tantrum over his absorption with his beloved car. It had never occurred to her that Marcus might suffer lasting hurt when she dismissed the magic of their night together as a mere nothing.

Julia hugged her arms about herself in desperation. What did any of it matter now? If the plane Marcus was flying home in had crashed in the fog all this would be academic. Of course, on the surface her life would be no different from the way it was before she had met Marcus. She would still have Sam. Only now she would have the memory of that night in the snowbound hotel to haunt her for the rest of her life, as a vision of what might have been.

She badly needed someone to talk to, someone to share her anxiety. But she made it a rule never to intrude on Laura and Tris more than she could help in the evenings, and consequently she wandered about the quiet rooms like a lost soul, looking in on the sleeping Sam, willing the telephone to ring, yet dreading it might in case the news was bad. She shuddered, and made herself coffee she couldn't drink, watched a television programme which could have been in Greek for all she understood of it. The sound of the doorbell when it rang later rocketed her to her feet in painful anticipation, her disappointment so acute when she opened the door to Claire Lang instead of Marcus that she felt physically sick.

'I'm afraid it's only me,' said Claire, and took Julia by the arm, closing the door behind her. 'For heaven's sake don't pass out on me, Julia—there's nothing wrong! Marcus is safe. His plane was diverted to Luton in the fog, and it was a while before he could let us know.'

Julia tried to thank her visitor, but burst into tears instead, letting herself be comforted in Claire's arms as though she were a child.

'I'm so sorry,' she said huskily at last, as she blew her nose inelegantly. 'I was off my head with worry. And when I saw you I thought you'd come to tell me the worst.'

'I'm sorry,' said Claire in remorse. 'But I'm here for a purpose. I want you to go somewhere. Now.'

'At this time of night?' Julia stared at her aghast.

'Yes,' said Claire firmly. 'Here are my car keys. And this is the key to Marcus's house. Now don't start raising all sorts of objections. Just be there waiting for him when he gets in. Garrett said not to interfere, but I just won't stand by and watch two adults making a pig's breakfast of their lives when a tiny push from a helping hand will put things right.'

And to her amazement, fifteen minutes later Julia found herself driving along the road to Marcus's house, while Claire stayed in Chester Road with Sam.

When she arrived at her destination Julia's heart thumped as she saw lights on in the house Claire's directions indicated was the right one, until it dawned on her that an electronics engineer like Marcus Lang would naturally have his lighting system working on a timing mechanism. The house stood some distance away from the road behind walls topped with laurel hedges, and she turned carefully into the drive, parking the car to the side of the house as Claire had instructed. Feeling horribly furtive, she let herself into the house and stood looking about her with wistful interest. Marcus had taste, she conceded. The stripped wood floors and thin, glowing rugs were just what she would have chosen herself for the solidly built Edwardian house, and when she opened a door on the room where Claire had suggested she wait, she knew it was where Marcus spent most of his time.

Antique pieces lived happily side by side with well-made modern furniture, most of it functional, and all of it beautiful, the muted colours contributing to the general impression of comfort and taste. Julia sat down in a winged chair in a corner near a bookcase which held old favourites of her own among the latest bestsellers and rows of technical tomes. She felt too much like an intruder to relax, afraid that Marcus might resent her presence in his home, almost sure by now he would want nothing more to do with her. Claire had given her enough time to change from her jeans and jersey into a red wool dress she had often worn to the office at Lang's, but she knew she looked pale and strained, and nowhere near her best. She was almost on the point of running away without waiting to see Marcus, when she heard a car draw up outside and the sound of doors slamming and Marcus's voice wishing someone goodnight.

Julia shrank back into the chair as she listened to him letting himself in, the thump of his suitcase on the floor in the hall before he opened the door and walked wearily into the room, making his way straight to the tray of drinks which stood on the sofa table. His back was half-turned to her as he poured himself a stiff, neat whisky and drank it in almost one swallow. He set it down on the tray and rotated his head wearily on his neck in the mannerism Julia knew so well. She watched, throat constricted, as he ran a hand through his hair, then reached again for the whisky decanter. He stopped, frozen, his arm in mid-air, then he spun round, his face incredulous as he saw her.

'*You?*' he said, then blinked hard and shook his head, staring at her again as though he couldn't believe his eyes. 'Is it really you, or am I dreaming?'

Julia got up and walked towards him. 'It's me right enough, Marcus.'

'How—I mean, *why* are you here?' he asked blankly.

'I've got a bone to pick with you,' she said, and stood with her arms folded, her eyes belligerent in response to the surprise in his. 'I've come to ask you what the hell you think you're playing at by refusing to give me a reference, Marcus Lang!'

It was just about the last thing she had intended to say once he arrived, but the words tumbled out in anger, as abruptly she found she was furious with him now she knew he was all right, like a mother with the child who has just escaped being run over. Now Marcus was here, safe, and not lying dead in the wreckage of a plane somewhere, she wanted to lash out at him.

Marcus looked dazed. 'You mean you've come here at this time of night to ask me that? And while we're on the subject, how did you get in?'

'Claire gave me the key.'

'*Claire?*'

They stood in the middle of the warm, beautiful room like a pair of gladiators about to do battle.

'You refused to give Mr Hetherington a reference when he asked for one,' said Julia heatedly. 'So naturally I didn't get the job! If you won't give me a reference how do you expect Sam and me to live, Marcus Lang!'

'I want you to come back to me,' he said simply, taking the wind out of her sails. 'I don't want you to work for someone else.'

Julia eyed him suspiciously. 'You mean you want me to come back and work for you?'

'No! I want you to *marry* me, you witless girl!' Marcus flung away and poured himself a whisky with an un-steady hand.

'Because of Sam, you mean?' Julia winced as she heard his teeth grind in frustration.

'No! Not because of Sam. Not that Sam isn't im-portant. But can't you get it through your head that even if Sam had never existed I would still want you to marry me?' He swung round and faced her, looking ashen and tired, his eyes bloodshot as they glared into hers. 'Is it so hard to believe? Did I imagine the sheer wonder of that night we shared? And I don't mean just the act itself, but the closeness and—and the sheer rightness of just being together!'

Julia bit her lip, and looked away. 'How did I know you felt like that? Next morning all you could think about was your stupid car.'

Marcus reached out and grabbed her by the elbows. 'Do you mean to say that *that*'s what this is all about? You went home in a huff because of the bloody Ferrari?'

Put like that it sounded wretchedly petty, and Julia nodded miserably, refusing to look up at him.

'Look at me!' he commanded. '*Look* at me, Julia.'

Reluctantly she raised her head and met his eyes.

'Did you never consider *my* feelings that morning?' he said passionately. 'Have you no idea what it did to me when you dismissed the whole thing as—as *nothing* next day?'

'No,' whispered Julia miserably.

'It may interest you to learn that my self-esteem shrivelled up and died,' he said, shaking her slightly. 'It hadn't been in very good shape ever since Nicola went off and left me with hardly a word of warning. Then the other morning, after what I'd rated as a trip to paradise, you behaved as though it was something to sweep under the carpet! I felt as though I'd been weighed in your personal little balance and found wanting—in your bed, in your life, in everything,' he said harshly.

Julia's eyes widened. 'Oh, no, Marcus, it wasn't like that at all!'

'No?' He looked sceptical. 'Then tell me how it was.'

'I was—upset,' she began with difficulty. 'I mean, about your running off to see to the car without so much as a word that morning. Then we met those men from marketing, and something which had been so wonderful suddenly seemed furtive and grubby. And I suppose I took it out on you.'

Marcus nodded grimly. 'I see. You did a great job, Julia.'

'I never thought for a moment you'd—you'd take it as final,' she went on doggedly. 'Everything I thought I knew about you indicated that—well, if you really wanted me you'd take no notice of what I said—realise I didn't mean it.'

He released her and drank some of the whisky, then belatedly offered her a drink. Julia shook her head.

'No, thank you,' she said stiffly. 'I must go. It was very silly of me to come here in the first place. Only I'd been off my head with worry, and——'

'Why?' he said quickly. 'Something wrong with Sam?'

'No.' Her eyes flashed suddenly. 'I happened to be worried because your plane was late, Marcus Lang. Or is that too hard for you to take in!'

He slammed down the glass on the tray, then seized her in his arms so suddenly she let out a squeak of fright.

'If I'm to reach complete understanding, Julia, I think you should let me know exactly what you mean. Persuade me that you mean what you say.'

Suddenly she could stand no more. She stood on tiptoe and slid her arms round his neck. 'I was off my head because I thought I'd never see you again, had never let you know I love you, Marcus Lang. Because I do. An hour or so ago I'd have sold my soul just to have you come back to me.'

Marcus gave a smothered groan and brought his mouth down on hers, his arms threatening to crack her ribs as he dragged her against him.

Julia began to cry, her tears drenching them both as she returned his kisses, hugging him as close as she could in response. 'I'm sorry I was horrible at first,' she said brokenly, when she could speak, and rubbed her cheek against his rough jaw over and over again, needing the touch of him to convince her he was alive and in her arms as she had longed for him to be for days and nights on end. 'But I'd been worried. I was shattered when Garrett told me your plane was overdue, then when I actually saw you I—I lost my temper.'

Marcus sat down on the sofa with her on his lap, looking a different man from the one who had first arrived. 'What fools we've been,' he said, and held her close, then laughed a little, unsteadily. 'Good thing none of my employees can see us now—the classic situation—secretary on boss's knee!'

Julia pulled free a little to look up at him, sniffing, her eyes narrowed. 'Who's your secretary now? Some long-legged blonde?'

Marcus grinned. 'Another widow, actually. Rather handsome in an austere way and at least ten years older than me. She'd probably bite my head off if I even called her by her first name.'

'Perfect!' Julia kissed him fiercely, and he caught his breath and returned the kiss with interest. The kiss went on and on, until they were both shaking.

'I want you so badly, darling,' he muttered urgently against her parted lips. 'Not just physically, but because for a moment or two in that plane I realised I might never see you again. I want you with me all night, to hold you in my arms, and know that we're both alive and together.'

Julia shook in his arms, returning his kisses feverishly, forgetting everything for a few wild moments.

'Let me ring Claire,' whispered Marcus. 'She'll stay with Sam.'

She was deeply tempted, but in the end she shook her head. 'No, darling,' she said unsteadily, 'we can't do that.'

He groaned and held her close. 'Julia, I want you so much it hurts. How the hell can I bring myself to let you go?'

'Come home with me and—and spend the night with me at my house, then,' said Julia in a rush, before she could think twice about it.

Marcus stared at her in astonishment, then gradually his breathing slowed and he followed the curve of her mouth lovingly with a fingertip. 'I'll go home with you, darling, but only to collect Claire. Thank you for the generous offer, but I think I've got enough willpower—

just—to hang on until we can spend every night together in legal wedlock, my darling. Only for goodness' sake let's make it soon!'

'Garrett said you've been like a bear with a sore head,' said Julia, still recovering from her uncharacteristic impulse.

'Oh, did he!' Marcus grinned. 'Then if you have any pity for your former colleagues at Lang's, I suggest you marry me a.s.a.p., Mrs North.' He stopped and looked deep into her eyes, his expression making her heart hammer. 'You'll never know how much I've wanted to change that name of yours to Lang, Julia.'

'Do you mind that I've been married before?' she asked bluntly.

'How can I? It's the second time for me too. I assure you, darling, that as long as you marry me this time I don't think I'll mind anything ever again!'

'Ah, you say that now, but what happens when you find out how cross I can be in the mornings——'

'How about the nights?'

'Let's not think about those right now,' she said shakily. 'And don't forget you'll have to share me with another demanding male, Marcus!'

'I can hardly blame you for that,' he said, and looked at her searchingly. 'Is all that really behind us now, Julia? Have you honestly forgiven me?'

Julia smiled at him and touched a hand to his unshaven cheek. 'Yes. You see, I always thought Garrett was the villain, anyway. Illogical, I suppose, but I've never really been able to transfer my feelings of vengeance to you, darling. Besides, Laura told me I was hopeless in the role of Nemesis.'

Marcus kissed her tenderly. 'She's right. The role you were destined for is wife to one lucky so-and-so by the name of Marcus Lang, sweetheart.'

She sighed, and wriggled closer to him. 'I think I'll play that to perfection—perfect typecasting!' She looked up at him squarely. 'And while we're on the subject, I'd just like to rid you of any doubts you might still possess about my opinion of our night together.'

Marcus tightened his hold involuntarily. 'Well?' he demanded.

'It was so unexpected.'

'Unexpected?'

She nodded. 'Because it was so—so light-hearted, and such *fun*, somehow. Until the last bit,' she added, colouring.

He eyed her with interest. 'And what was that like?'

'The most wonderful experience of my life.'

After which Marcus expressed his appreciation of her compliment with such passionate fervour it was a long time before either of them remembered that life was going on as usual in the outside world.

At last, reluctantly, he agreed it was time to let Claire know all was well, and drive Julia home.

'My darling sister-in-law can drop me off on her way back to Rigg Farm,' he said with satisfaction as they set off. 'We owe Claire a great big vote of thanks.'

'Would you really have stayed away from me if she hadn't stepped in?' asked Julia.

'No, of course not. I was just letting you suffer a bit,' he said smugly.

'Oh, were you?'

'No,' he amended quickly. 'It was I who was suffering, Julia. But I couldn't have kept away any longer.

I was prepared to do anything you wanted, just so long as you came back to me.'

As they reached the town a few flakes of snow began to drift down, and Julia smiled, rubbing her cheek against his sleeve. 'I'll always love snow from now on. I'll never see it without thinking of the night we were snowed up together in that lovely little hotel.'

'If snow has the same effect every time I vote we go to the Alps for our honeymoon,' suggested Marcus, as he stopped the car at her gate.

Julia looked at him doubtfully. 'I've never done any skiing, Marcus.'

He gathered her into his arms and kissed her hard, chuckling as he slid his lips across her cheek to her ear. 'Who said anything about skiing?'

VOWS   *LaVyrle Spencer*   £2.99

When high-spirited Emily meets her father's new business rival,
Tom, sparks fly, and create a blend of pride and passion in this
compelling and memorable novel.

LOTUS MOON   *Janice Kaiser*   £2.99

This novel vividly captures the futility of the Vietnam War and the
legacy it left. Haunting memories of the beautiful Lotus Moon fuel
Buck Michael's dangerous obsession, which only Amanda Parr can
help overcome.

SECOND TIME LUCKY   *Eleanor Woods*   £2.75

Danielle has been married twice. Now, as a young, beautiful widow,
can she back-track to the first husband whose life she left in ruins
with her eternal quest for entertainment and the high life?

**These three new titles will be out in bookshops from
September 1989.**

W●RLDWIDE

*Available from Boots, Martins, John Menzies, W.H. Smith, Woolworths
and other paperback stockists.*

Experience the thrill of 4 Mills & Boon Romances

FREE BOOKS FOR YOU

Enjoy all the heartwarming emotions of true love.
The dawning of a passion too great for you to control. The
uncertainties and the heartbreak. And then, when it seems
almost too late - the ecstasy that knows no bounds!

Now you can enjoy four captivating Romances as a **free** gift
from Mills & Boon, plus
the chance to have
6 Romances delivered
to your door every
single month.

**Turn the page for details of 2 extra
free gifts, and how to apply**

An irresistible offer from Mills & Boon

Here's a personal invitation from Mills & Boon to become a regular reader of Romance. And to welcome you, we'd like you to have four books, an enchanting pair of glass oyster dishes and a special MYSTERY GIFT.

Then each month you could look forward to receiving 6 more brand – new Romances, delivered to your door, post and packing **free**. Plus our newsletter featuring author news, competitions and special offers.

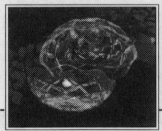

This invitation comes with no strings attached. You can stop or suspend your subscription at any time, and still keep your **free** books and gifts.

It's so easy. Send no money now. Simply fill in the coupon below at once and post it to -

Reader Service, FREEPOST, P.O Box 236, Croydon, Surrey. CR9 9EL

- - -✂- - - - - - - - - *No stamp required* - - - - - -

YES! Please rush me my 4 Free Romances and 2 FREE gifts!

Please also reserve me a Reader Service Subscription. If I decide to subscribe, I can look forward to receiving 6 brand new Romances each month, for just £8.10 delivered direct to my door. Post and packing is **free**. If I choose not to subscribe I shall write to you within 10 days - I can keep the books and gifts whatever I decide. I can cancel or suspend my subscription at any time.
I am over 18.

EP61R

NAME _____

ADDRESS _____

_____

_____ *POSTCODE* _____

SIGNATURE _____